A Birth at Dawn

Also by Christie Silvers:
Toddler Logic: 50 Things That Your Toddler Wants You to Know

The Alex & Fiona Series:
A Midnight Infatuation

A Birth at Dawn

Christie Silvers

First edition April 2008

A BIRTH AT DAWN

© 2008 Christie Silvers

ISBN 978-0-6152-0458-1

Cover Image Copyright © 2007 Zindy S. D. Nielsen

All Rights Reserved. http://zindy.zone.dk

zindy@zone.dk

Cover Design by Mis Smith

http://www.MisMadeDesigns.com

For more information about this book or its author visit http://www.christiesilvers.com.

ACKNOWLEDGMENTS

Thank you to everyone who read *A Midnight Infatuation*. I hope that you will enjoy this book as much as the last. I enjoyed writing it, and look forward to the next chapter in the lives of Alex and Fiona.

Thank you to my dear friend, Mis. I am so glad that we know each other now and I wish we'd met sooner.

Prologue

As you may already know, I am Fiona. I'm a werewolf who was killed by her pack. Luckily, I had a secret admirer who just happened to be a vampire. He saved me on the night of my death. He defeated my killer and brought me back to life by turning me.

Unfortunately, a werewolf had never been turned by a vampire and we didn't know what types of changes or problems to expect. Hell, we didn't even know the other species actually existed before that night. We've had an interesting ride together, to say the least.

*   *   *   *

It's me again, Alexander. I'm the vampire who is in love with the lovely Fiona. She is the love of my life and I can't even fathom how I survived my 150 years without her in my life. The night that she died was the best night of my undead existence—or my live existence, at that.

We went through a lot in the first month that we were together. Fiona had some family "issues" to work through and I'd like to think that I helped her during all of it. So what if those issues meant that she had to kill a whole wolf pack council. They shouldn't have killed her first.

Chapter 1

"You've got to be kidding me!"

Diane was beyond surprised when I told her what had happened those weeks after I left her a phone message telling her good-bye. I had planned that message to be the last that Diane would hear from me, because my pack had intended upon killing me that night— Thanksgiving night to be exact. Luckily, I had attracted quite an interesting admirer and he saved my life that night. He just so happened to be a vampire who had to turn me in order to save me.

"God Diane, would you stop saying that and help me pick out a damn dress? I only have two weeks before the wedding and I can't find anything that looks right with this belly all pooching out like it is."

It was Saturday, April 13th and we were in the *Got a Dress? Wedding Boutique*—which was, unfortunately, the closest place to buy a great wedding dress in such a short amount of time—and I was digging through rack after rack of multi-colored, overly poufy, and ridiculously priced wedding dresses. This store was a typical wedding boutique, with typical, obnoxious, and annoying salesgirls hovering around constantly asking if they can help me. All I wanted to do was find a damn dress and get this over with, but they wanted to "show" me this dress or that dress—all so obviously NOT my taste.

Alex and I had planned a lovely spring wedding, and while every last detail had been completed weeks ago, my wedding dress choice was still circling my head like a vulture waiting for me to die of dehydration. I only had two weeks left before our wedding day and Diane had promised to help me find the perfect dress. Unfortunately, we had been in this damn store for six hours today, and that doesn't count the four hours I was in here by myself yesterday, and the numerous times Alex had stopped in without me. I keep telling him that I have to choose the dress, but he knows how I hate this kind of stuff.

"I just can't believe it! I know that you've been retelling this tale of yours for the last few weeks, but it's just so amazing that I can't believe it."

Diane had been flabbergasted ever since the first time I told her about Alex and me. Well, actually she hadn't even known about Alex, much less about an Alex and me. She had only heard a cryptic phone message saying that I was going to die, and that I would miss her. So when I showed up on her doorstep—alive and pregnant— she was beyond shocked.

"You can believe that I'm a werewolf and you can still be my best friend from childhood, and yet you can't believe that Alex is a vampire, he turned me, and now I'm pregnant with his child?" I laughed while shaking my head in disbelief and she snickered at my statement.

"Well damn Fiona, when you say it like that…," she scoffed. "It's just a little unbelievable. First off, I never imagined that vampires were REAL. Then, you go and fall in love with one and proceed to get knocked up with his love child. How the hell can he get you pregnant to begin with? He's DEAD! Right?"

"You know that I've already explained that to you… about twenty times!" I could never get pissed with Diane, but my hormonal nerves were fried at this point and I looked up at her from the rack of dresses and gave her my patented *Go to Hell* look.

"Ok, ok, I'm sorry. It's just crazy weird. Of course I believe you, and you know that I'm always here for you. I just wish you had told me about all of this sooner, instead of springing it on me after I thought you were dead and I'd lost my best friend."

She came over to me and hugged me tight. When we released each other, I look into her eyes and smiled. I had missed her terribly while I was struggling with my pack. As soon as I found out I was pregnant I knew that I needed my friend at my side during this adventure.

"Ok, ok. Diane, you know I love you like a sister, but I really need you to help me out here. What do you think of this?" I asked.

I held up an off-white, off the shoulders, silk gown that flowed from waist to ankles like waves on the ocean. It had long sleeves and would accentuate my breasts beautifully (I never imagined that pregnancy would provide so much more ampleness in the chest area). It wasn't form-fitting—which is great when you have an ever-expanding abdomen—and after being in the store for six hours I was ready to choose and get the hell out of here.

"Oooohhh, I LOVE IT! You definitely need to try that one on. What size is it?"

I glanced down at the small slip of white paper hanging from the sleeve of my perfect dress and discovered that it was a size ten. Exactly the size I needed! This dress couldn't be more perfect if someone had stood here and sewn it for me right in front of my eyes.

I showed the tag to Diane and she smiled widely. Her toothy smile always reminds me of a certain red-headed actress who has always been gorgeous. Standing side by side, Diane was about an inch taller than me, but it's really just her huge hair. She likes it "fluffy", as she puts it.

In a flash she was grabbing the dress and running for the cashier. "I'm buying this for you. Consider it a wedding gift from your best friend" she shouted across the room.

"Oh, no you're not! I don't want you to buy my dress. Besides, Alex has PLENTY of money and told me to buy whatever I wanted." But, my words feel on deaf ears. She was so fast that I couldn't catch up to her before the cashier had swiped her credit card, and the deal was done.

As we walked out of the store—her with a giant smile on her face and I with a wedding dress tossed over my arm—I felt a great sense of happiness. I always felt that way when I was with Alex or when I was thinking of the little life that was growing inside of me, but it had been a while since I'd felt that with a friend... ever since I killed Jeffrey. Ah, Jeffrey.

The thought of my best Were-friend, turned betrayer, made me sad, but Diane would have none of that. She tugged me down the sidewalk toward one of my favorite coffee shops. This place had every kind of coffee drink imaginable, and a few you wouldn't imagine. But, my favorite item on the menu wasn't coffee, it was their strawberry cheesecake danish. YUM!

"Come on sweetie, let me lavish you with danish", Diane said cheerfully. "I know you love the stuff and that little baby...," she patted my ever expanding waistline, "needs the nourishment."

"Ah Diane, you know how to make a girl feel special." I chuckled, and we headed into the coffee shop where I proceeded to down three strawberry cheesecake danishes and an extra large cup of orange juice. This, in turn, caused me to have to rush to the bathroom before the weight of the baby made my bladder to explode.

When I returned to the table, Diane had a serious look on her face. She was no longer cheerful and enthusiastic. She was now worried, cautious, and concerned.

"What? What have I done now?" I questioned.

"Nothing. I was just thinking." She paused, ran her hand through her "fluffy" hair and then fiddled with her fingernails. This usually meant that she wanted to ask me something, but wasn't sure how I'd react to it.

"What is it, Diane? I know you have something on your mind, so get on with it." I sipped my orange juice and waited patiently for Diane to spill what ever was on her mind. She wouldn't be able to hold out for long.

"Well, sweetie, you know that I love you like a sister. You have been my best friend since the day we met all those years ago." I nodded in agreement and she continued, "I'm just worried about you. You've been through so much in the last few months, and well, I'm afraid that if you stay with this man you, and your child, will only suffer more in the years to come."

I couldn't believe what I was hearing. Diane was afraid for my safety. She was worried about my child's safety. I was surprised, and a little angry.

"You're worried? About me? Why in the hell would you be worried about the baby and me? And what does it have to do with Alex? He's been nothing but wonderful to me and he's completely in love with the idea of our child coming into this world. There's absolutely nothing to worry about. Alex would never hurt me, or Isabella."

The volume of my voice was beginning to rise from the thoughts that Diane would dare accuse Alex of harming the baby or me. "And if you think for one minute that I'm going to leave Alex just because you say so, then you are sadly mistaken.... best friends or not!"

Diane saw the fire in my eyes and she didn't speak for a moment. She simply laid her hands upon mine and squeezed reassuringly. She let me calm down before she spoke again.

"Fiona, honey, please don't get upset. I didn't mean that Alex would hurt you or baby Isabella. I just meant that being with him can't be safe. Not because of HIM, but possibly because of the people he knows. If one vampire exists, then we can be certain that there are many more out there, and they may not be as friendly as your man is."

"You're kidding, right? You are seriously concerned about Alex being able to protect me, when my own pack tried to kill me? Alex was the one who saved me from never living another day on this earth! He would never allow anything to happen to me."

I thought for a second and realized that I didn't need Alex to protect me anyway. "Diane, don't you remember me telling you about how I killed the werewolf council—the ENTIRE werewolf council? Don't you think that I can take care of myself if push comes to shove? I didn't need Alex to protect me then, and I don't need his protection now."

Diane looked truly sorry that she had spoken badly against Alex. "I'm sorry, Fiona. I never meant to upset you. I only wanted to make sure that you're going to be taken care of. I don't want to go through the death of my best friend, again. I know that you can take care of yourself, even before you were turned, but I don't want little Isabella to be stuck in the middle of a dangerous battle between Alex and some other vampire. Or worse off, some other creature we didn't know existed."

"Diane, don't worry about Isabella. Her father and I will never let anything happen to her." With that, I smiled at Diane and she reciprocated.

"Now, let's get back to this wedding mess. Did you have your dress fitting yesterday? Is everything alright with your dress?" And that was the end of Diane's worries about my safety... or at least I hoped it was.

"Oh yes, the dress is beautiful and fits perfectly. I can't wait for the wedding so that I can wear it. You know that I'll be the best looking woman at the whole wedding..."

She paused and I gave her a raised eyebrow before she continued, "with the exception of the bride of course!" We roared with laughter and everyone in the coffee shop looked our way. We tried to stifle our giggles while collecting our bags and heading for the door.

I stepped out the door of the coffee shop and a chill ran up my spine. I had the feeling like someone was watching me. My eyes quickly darted up and down the sidewalk, but I didn't see anyone. The street was empty, except for a stray dog and a runaway newspaper that was twirling in the wind.

But, I knew that someone was there, and I always trusted my instincts these days. Ever since the night that my pack sent a bounty hunter after me, I'd been more in tune to the world around me. I wouldn't be caught off guard again, especially now that I had Isabella to protect.

I was so focused on the possibility of someone spying on me that it startled me when Diane walked up behind me and asked, "Are you alright? You look very pale all of a sudden. Is it the morning sickness again? Do you need to rest?"

"No, I'm alright." I looked up and down the street once more. "I think I'm ready to head home for the day. Alex will be awake in a few hours and I'll need to feed. Isabella isn't happy if I skip even one feeding."

Diane snarled her nose up in disgust. "I'll never get use to the idea that you 'feed'. The thought of you drinking blood makes my stomach churn."

I laughed at her. "Well, you do remember that I'm a werewolf, right? I use to feed on wild animals during every full moon. Only now it's more fun because the sex is awesome!"

This time it was Diane who raised her eyebrows. I winked and then hugged her good-bye before walking in the direction of my car.

Chapter 2

It was early in the evening and I had just awakened to the sound of my sweet Fiona singing in the new shower that I recently installed for her. She had been asking me to add another bathroom downstairs in the master suite, so that she wouldn't have to run upstairs every time she wanted to take a shower. I was happy to oblige because I didn't want her left vulnerable upstairs anymore. At least down here she could lock herself in and no one would be able to get to her. We wouldn't have another attempt on her life like last year.

I snuck into the bathroom—which was only a small bathroom with a sink, toilet, and shower stall—and tried to slip into the shower without Fiona knowing. But, since she's half werewolf I can never sneak up on her.

"I hear you. Stop trying to slip up on me and just get in here." I could hear her snickering over the sound of the running water. I slipped into the shower and saw her washing her face. Her eyes were closed, but she knew I was there.

I slid my hands down her back and caressed her firm behind. She slowly turned around and I was graced with the lovely view of her expanding belly. I kneeled down and circled my hands around that little bump before kissing her stomach right above the navel. I laid my ear against her and spoke to my child within.

"Good evening my sweet Isabella. Have you been kind to your mommy today?"

Fiona ran her fingers through my hair and when I looked up, she had the most beautiful smile on her lips. I love it when she smiles like that. I had never seen a smile so lovely before I saw it on Fiona's face.

"She's been pretty good today. She's been wiggling around and kicking me in the bladder, but other than that we're good. How was your day? Did you sleep well?"

I knew what she was trying to do. She was trying to take my mind off of what her task was for the day. She had promised to find the perfect wedding dress today. The wedding was a mere two weeks away and the dress was all we were waiting on.

I stood up, kissed her soft lips while water was showering down upon us, and then I ran my tongue down the right side of her neck. She moaned with arousal as I hit that one special spot on her neck that she loves so much. She leaned her head to the left and I took that as an approval to do what I wanted with her.

I slid my hands around her back, grabbed her buttocks, pressed my body against her, and then I bit into that throbbing vein on her neck with enough fierceness that she gasped with surprise. I love it when she does that, and she doesn't seem to mind. It reminds me of the old days when I would take what I wanted from any woman around—now I only wanted it from my Fiona.

Fiona was moaning and I could feel the member between my legs begin to awaken from its slumber. I carefully lifted her hips and she promptly wrapped her legs around my waist. I positioned her back against the shower wall and we pumped back and forth until the rays of ecstasy were right over the horizon.

I released my hold on Fiona's neck. She looked into my eyes and smiled so widely that I could see her own fangs protruding. It was her turn and I felt so impatient that I pressed my neck right to her mouth. She giggled because she knew that as soon as she bit into my neck I would reach my peak and it would be over. She wanted to torment me.

She licked my neck, nipped at the flesh, and then grabbed two handfuls of my hair and forcibly pulled my head to one side before piercing the skin with her fangs. I heard a moan escape from my own throat when the flesh tore. I pumped harder until she stopped feeding and we were both about to explode.

We moaned one last time in unison before she screamed and her whole body went into spasms. I felt her body tighten around mine and I couldn't hold it back any longer. My seed spewed forth into her moist, warm body and a wave of relaxation flowed over us both.

"Ahhh, that was incredible" she purred into my ear while panting to catch her breath.

She was still straddling me, and I didn't want to release her. She kissed me sweetly and rubbed the tips of her fingers down my back; her nails lightly scratching the flesh on their way down. She leaned over and licked the blood that was streaming down my own neck. Her tongue wagged ever so slowly over the wounds and my loins tingled with so much delight that a shiver ran up my spine.

The wounds on my neck healed and I lowered her onto her own feet. We both rinsed off and retreated from the shower. I was drying her smooth body when my hands settled on her swollen abdomen. She was so warm and my cold hands loved it.

My hands circled that little bump and then I placed my right hand directly over Fiona's navel. My hand had only been there for about ten seconds when our daughter made her presence known. She kicked with such veracity that Fiona gasped and clasped her hands over mine.

"Be a good girl in there, Isabella. Mommy can't take many of those karate chops." Fiona smiled while she chastised our unborn daughter.

After we got dressed, we went upstairs and settled down in front of the fireplace. I'm always cold, but Fiona is so warm-natured that she started to complain about the temperature. I didn't feel like talking about that subject, yet again, so I changed the subject.

"So how did dress shopping go today? Find anything special, or are we going to see you walking down the aisle naked? Not that I would mind!"

She looked at me like she could kill me. Then, her face lightened and she smiled her big, bright smile and shouted, "I FOUND IT!!" Her voice was full of glee when she continued, "I found the most perfect dress today and it only took six hours in the same damn store we've been rummaging through for weeks now."

"That's fantastic. I was afraid that you'd never find something you liked." I really was glad that she'd finally found a dress. The hunt for this thing was starting to tire me.

Suddenly, she got this worried expression on her face. "What's wrong? Do you have to get it altered, or was it the wrong size? Do you need more money to get it... because I'll be happy to give you some more!"

"No, no, Diane bought me the dress as a gift. It's in the closet. AND, NO YOU CAN'T SEE IT", she shouted after me as I rushed to the hall closet. Just as I was opening the door she caught up with me and slammed it closed; nearly taking my index finger with it.

"Aw, come on, let me have a look." There was that look on her face again. If looks could kill, she'd corner the market on assassinations.

"NO! Leave the dress alone. You know that it's bad luck and we don't need more bad luck after last year. I don't want to have to kill another room full of people, especially while I'm pregnant."

16

"Alright then, I'll leave it be. But, why do you look so worried? The wedding is all planned and you've finally found you dress. There's nothing else left to do, aside from getting hitched."

We walked back over to the couch and she snuggled against me before staring into the flickering flames dancing over the wooden logs in the fireplace. I could tell that something was bothering her, but it would take some gentle coaxing to get it out of her. She could be stubborn at times, especially when it comes to dangerous situations.

"What is it my love? You can tell me anything, and you know that. Is it the baby? Is something wrong? Oh, please don't tell me there's something wrong with the baby!"

"No, nothing is wrong with the baby. I just had a check-up with Samantha a few days ago. Everything looks fine with our baby girl. No worries, Alex."

"Then what's going on?"

She turned to face me, fidgeted with her hands, smoothed her hair, and then rubbed her stomach. She really didn't want to tell me whatever it was she knew. I was starting to get worried.

"Come on sweetie. Tell me what's wrong."

"Ok. Well, I was having a snack with Diane at the coffee shop. You know the one... it has those delicious cheesecake danishes that I love so much." I nodded. "Well, when we started to leave, a strange feeling came over me." She paused a moment before continuing, "A feeling like someone was watching me; someone who didn't want to be seen."

"Maybe it was just someone enjoying the beauty of a pregnant woman. Or maybe it's a hormonal thing."

"Alex, don't play this off as nothing, especially after everything we've been through. I KNOW what I felt and I KNOW that someone was watching me. The question is... WHO?"

"I'm sorry. I'm not trying to play it off. I'm just worried that you're a little overly-sensitive in your present condition. Samantha did say that she wasn't sure how the pregnancy would affect your senses and emotions since it's a cross-breed conception."

Fiona stood up from the couch and headed to the kitchen. I got up to follow and she yelled back, "Don't bother. I'm just getting some water."

I went to the kitchen anyway. She was standing over the sink sipping water from a glass. I started to walk up behind her, but before I made it to her she dropped the glass and I watched it fall before it shattered into a million tiny shards of glass all over the tile floor. When I looked back up, Fiona was doubled over and cradling her stomach like the precious cargo it was.

I flew over to her and lifted her into my arms. Her face was pale and twisted in pain. I didn't say a word—I just rushed out the door and took to the sky. I had only one thing in mind when we left the cottage; get my beloved straight to Doctor Samantha's office.

Chapter 3

I awoke to the smell vanilla—which was a big upgrade from the antiseptic and plastic that I had smelled in the hospital for the last week and a half. We had quite the pregnancy scare, but Alex got me to Samantha's office within minutes. I hope that I'll be able to fly as quickly as he could some day.

Baby Isabella is doing fine; I just had some very strong Braxton Hicks contractions that were completely unexpected. But to be on the safe side, Samantha kept me in the hospital for observation. Oh, and don't worry about my werewolf/vampire secret getting out. Samantha has her own "special" staff of medical professionals that only take care of her patients.

Anyway, today was going to be the biggest day of my life. It was Saturday, April 27th and it was my thirty-first birthday. Not only that, but it was also the day that I would be marrying the man of my dreams. It had been five months since the night I sensed Alex's presence outside the Stop 'n Go. It had been five months since I died. And it had been five months since I got pregnant with our miracle child.

In these last five months some extraordinary events have occurred. My werewolf DNA has revived Alex's dead body. He was still a vampire, only now he has live sperm (obviously) and he is growing hair again; he actually has to shave now! His hair doesn't grow as fast as mine, or even as fast as a normal human's, but it is growing. He's had a farmer's son hair cut since he was turned (turns out he WAS a farmer's son when he was alive) and now he has enough hair for me to grab during those...um...."special" moments.

When I awoke, I turned and looked into the face of this handsome hunk of a man. He was facing me in his dead sleep—he always snuggles up against me when we go down for the day. I smiled at the serene expression on his beautiful face. I love him so much and can't imagine where I would be if I had never met him. Well, actually, I would be dead if I hadn't met him, so I guess that every day I'm alive is a gift from Alex, himself.

I caressed his cheek; it was cold as ice, but it had a rough layer of stubble that pricked my hand. I miss his smooth skin, but he seems to enjoy the mundane routine of cutting this hair off of his jawline everyday. It makes him feel more human, I suppose.

He didn't even twitch when I touched him. He really is dead when he's sleeping. Nothing can wake him when the sun is high in the sky. I sometimes feel lonely during the sunlight hours.

Even though I'm half vampire, my werewolf DNA is more prominent. Therefore, I am able to be up and around during the daytime. I like to stay up late with Alex, but sometimes a girl just needs some sunlight, especially on her wedding day!

I kissed Alex on the lips, rose from the bed and waddled (yes, I waddle these days) over to the new bathroom—Alex really is quite handy and was more than eager to build me a bathroom so that I didn't have to go upstairs all the time. As I was saying, I waddled into the bathroom, used the toilet (I'm still bummed about not getting out of doing such things), washed my face, and brushed my teeth—making sure to extend the fangs so they would be sparkly clean for the day.

I grabbed the loose-fitting maternity clothes that I'd hung on the back of the door the night before and proceeded to stuff myself into them. I felt Isabella squirm and stretch, so I rubbed my stomach and said, "Good morning my sweet. We have an exciting day planned for today. I hope that you will behave for me. We won't be able to feed from daddy until late, so some real food will have to sustain you for now."

This pregnancy has been very odd, to say the least. There has never been a vampire and werewolf conception. Hell, there's never been a vampire conception. So this is all a strange and new territory for everyone involved.

Since I am a werewolf, there are certain physical aspects of pregnancy that all werewolf females go through. If they have curly hair (like mine), it straightens (mine has). They won't change during full moons (which I haven't since I was turned anyway). They will hunger for bloody raw meats more regularly (I crave Alex's blood more regularly). And there is a particular urge for closeness from the male who impregnated them.

All of those things have occurred right on schedule. What's weird about this pregnancy is that most werewolf cubs are born in the spring. But, according to ultrasounds of the baby's growth, Samantha estimated my due date as the end of August. We are chalking it up to the small amount of human DNA that my blood had revived in Alex. It's basically a wait-and-see situation.

After brushing my hair, I started upstairs. I was halfway up the stairs when I glanced back at Alex. I had that feeling again, like someone was watching me. The last time a bad feeling washed over me in this same room, was the night I killed the werewolf council. I looked down at my stomach and whispered to myself, "There's no way I want to do anything like that in this condition." I looked back at Alex and wondered if Isabella would have his eyes.

The sun was shining brightly and it was a lovely spring afternoon. I walked outside with a steaming cup of hot chocolate (I'm trying to stay off the caffeine) and sat down in the Adirondack chair that Alex had built for me. The sunlight was streaming through the newly budding leaves on the tall forest trees. The birds were singing from their hidden perches. There was a soft breeze—just enough to make me shiver for a moment—and the sky was a gorgeous shade of pale blue.

I looked over at the empty matching chair across from me and wished that Alex was sitting there enjoying this moment with me. Just then Isabella wiggled and let me know that I wasn't alone and she was here with me. Like my morning sickness could ever let me forget. I scoffed at the thought.

Just then, I heard a car coming up the gravel driveway heading straight for me. Once it got around the curve and out of the forest trees, I saw that it was Diane's white mini-van. She was right on schedule to get things ready for the wedding—which was going to happen right here in the middle of this forest with all the woodland creatures as guests.

Diane bounced out of her vehicle and sauntered over to me. I didn't rise, but motioned for her to take the empty chair across from me (someone might as well sit in it). She took the seat and then said, "Whew! Do you think you live far enough out in the woods? My poor van wasn't built to go four-wheeling."

She smiled brightly and, without awaiting my reply, asked, "So are you ready? Are you so excited that you can't stand it? I remember when David and I got married. You remember how nervous, excited, and completely sick to my stomach I was? It was the most scary and exciting day of my life!"

She paused, thought for a moment, and then corrected her last statement with, "Well, that is until the births of my children. Now those days are scary."

"Well damn Diane, why don't you scare an expectant mother completely to death!" I was already nervous enough about giving birth and that's not including all of the possibilities of things going wrong because of the origins of this child.

Diane chuckled, winked at me, and then came over to hug me tightly. "I'm sorry sweetie. You will be perfectly fine and, of course, I'll be there to help you. Besides, today's about you and Alex uniting in matrimony! Are you ready to get started on this shin-dig?"

I took one last gulp of my hot chocolate and felt the warm liquid slide down the back of my throat and into my stomach. I waited a moment to see if it would stay there or if Isabella would reject it. Luckily it stayed put.

I stood up—Diane rushed over to pull me—and said, "Come on then. Let's get this party started!"

I started inside and Diane yelled that she had to get some things from her van. I said alright and continued inside. Suddenly, it hit me again... that feeling of being watched. I turned around and scanned the forest floor, the trees, and even the sky. The only movement I detected was Diane getting stuff from the back of her van.

She popped her head around the van and asked, "What's wrong? Do I need to call the doctor?"

"No, I'm alright. I just thought I heard something. Do you need any help?"

"Heck no, Preggo! You go inside. I'm just grabbing my dress and our To-Do list." Diane's *to-do list* was usually a binder filled to the brim. She never did anything simply.

I took one last, long look around the area before finally heading inside the cottage. I went to the kitchen for more hot chocolate and made Diane a cup of coffee. When she came inside, we settled down at the kitchen table to go over the list.

"Alright, we have to call the caterers and make sure that they are on their way. They should be, but let's make sure. Then we need to call the bakery and see if the cake is ready. You picked a beautiful cake. Did Alex like it?"

"Actually Alex picked the cake out... even though he won't be eating much of it. Not like I will anyway." We laughed and then Diane continued.

"Ok..." she ran her finger down the page and scanned quickly "we need to make sure the florist is on their way to create the altar. Do you still want to go with the flower crown?"

I nodded. The flower crown had been Alex's idea. He said that it came to him in a dream. Most of the wedding arrangements were Alex's idea. That's fine with me because I hate planning extravagant events.

"Well, there really isn't that much to do, especially now that you have the dress. I didn't think you'd ever find a dress", she chuckled.

"Let's get this started." I agreed, and we both jumped on our separate phones.

Within forty-five minutes we had both confirmed all of the necessary arrangements for the wedding. Everything was on schedule and within another thirty minutes people started showing up to create the wedding of my dreams. Well, actually it was of Alex's dreams, but that was ok with me.

A few hours later (after much gossiping, hot chocolate, and a nap), Diane and I walked out into the backyard to see what kind of progress had been made. I gasped from the beauty of what had been created. This simple forest-filled backyard had been turned into the most beautiful, woodland, wedding sanctuary that I had ever seen.

"Oh Diane, it's gorgeous!"

"Wait until you see it when the sun goes down. There are lights strung up in all of these trees and even throughout the flowers around the altar," Diane pointed out.

There was a long stretch of red carpet rolled out from the back door of the cottage up to the altar. On each side there were about a dozen white chairs. Up at the front, there was a wooden altar with a canopy of wild flowers over it. There were ribbons flowing over the tops of all the guests' chairs and small, twinkling lights strung throughout everything.

All around the parameter were tall candles sitting upon metal stands. These helped separate the forest from the wedding and they would help with illumination after the sun went down. Behind all of the chairs, there were buffet tables lined up with tent canopies over them. There were even lights hanging from the edges of the canopies. No one should have a problem seeing anything tonight.

The wedding was scheduled for nine o'clock that night and, since it was only five o'clock, we had a little while before the guests would start arriving. Alex would be waking in about two hours, so Diane and I had time to spend together before all the rush would begin. I suggested that we go start on my hair and she agreed.

We turned to head back inside, but then Diane said, "Oh, I almost forgot! This is for you." I looked and saw her holding the most exquisite crown made of wild flowers. There were numerous shades of purples, pinks, and blues entwined around each other. The florist had even made it so that there were a few strands of flowers hanging down the back that would intertwine with my hair.

"It's beautiful!" I exclaimed. "What a wonderful idea that Alex came up with."

I was so excited, but I couldn't shake the feeling that something or someone was going to be putting a kink in my plans for tonight. As long as it doesn't rain, I guess I can handle any situation. Besides, Alex will be by my side and we can take on the world together—or at least try!

Chapter 4

Ahhh, nightfall was finally here. My stomach was churning from
excitement. You'd think that after one hundred and fifty years there
wouldn't be many things in this undead existence that would excite
me, but tonight does. I've always wanted to have a wife and children,
but those desires were lost all those years ago on a spring night just
like tonight. But, I don't want to think about those distasteful
memories on a night as special as this. Not tonight.

I looked around the room to see if I would be lucky enough to
spot my bride-to-be before the ceremony, no such luck. It appeared
that she was holding to tradition about the groom not seeing the

bride before the wedding. Otherwise, she would be down here on top of me in a flash and I wouldn't mind one bit. I assumed that she was upstairs in one of the spare bedrooms.

I floated out of bed (yes, floated. I'm a vampire and I can float) and flew to the bathroom. I showered and shaved. I so enjoy shaving these days. I haven't done it since I was thirty years old and here I was coming up on one hundred and fifty-one. The technology in today's razors is amazing, but I tend to lean more toward the old barber shop straight blades of my youth.

After I was all cleaned up, I went back into the bedroom and saw that Fiona had laid out my tux. She had everything together and in order of what I should put on first. I was never one to wear a suit when I was alive and certainly hadn't aspired to do so after my death.

Looking at all of the intricate details of this outfit made me think of Serena. Serena had been my fiancée, when I was alive. She used to insist upon me wearing nice clothes when I was courting her. She was always disappointed when I showed up at her house, even though I was always in clean clothes—just not the kinds of clothes she wanted me to wear.

After that moment of remembrance, I went right to work getting dressed for the wedding day that I'd always wanted. This was the wedding that I had dreamed about all those months ago, before we knew that Fiona was pregnant and before I could have even imagined that Isabella could be a possibility. This would be a great night!

*   *   *   *

I looked at the clock and realized that Diane had been working on my hair for over and hour. My head was starting to ache and my stomach was starting to rumble from hunger—and not the kind of hunger that any food from the fridge would cure. But, my stomach would have to hold out until after the wedding.

"You look gorgeous, Fiona!" Diane was squealing from excitement. "Now, we need to get you into your dress. Have you tried it on since you brought it home? I hope so since I didn't give you time to do it at the store." Diane chuckled from remembering how she had beaten a pregnant woman in a foot race to the cash register.

"Thanks, Diane," I snickered. "Yes, I tried on the dress as soon as I got home that day. It's been hanging in the hall closet since then. Just run over there and get it for me, would ya?"

Without answering, Diane was out the door and darting across the living room to the hall closet. She left the spare bedroom's door open, so I could see her charging her way through the house. Just as she made it to the hall closet, Alex appeared out of nowhere.

"Noooo! You can NOT see me yet", I screamed out while rushing to close the bedroom door. As soon as it closed I yelled, "Diane, do NOT let him see that dress! Alex you go somewhere else. Do NOT look at my dress. It's bad luck!"

I had my ear against the wooden door, just waiting to hear him reply with some snide remark about me being silly, about how we were already together, and the wedding was just a ritual. But instead, I was surprised when he whispered through the door, "Ok my beloved. I'll do anything you want just as long as you are marrying me tonight. I can't wait to see you float toward me in your secret dress."

It was so sweet that tears welled up in my eyes and I heard Diane firmly remark, "Do NOT ruin her make-up with all that sappiness, Mr. Jenkins. You go on outside and let me get your bride presentable."

I could hear Alex do one of his deep belly laughs before he said, "Yes, my dear Diane. I will go outside. Fiona, I will await your arrival with bated breath. I love you, my beauty and tell our daughter that I love her too."

Before I could reply, Diane was bursting through the door and closing it just as quickly behind her. "Whew, that was close. I almost had the dress out of the closet when he just appeared. How did you ever get use to his sneakiness?"

"Ah, it's not that bad. His speed actually came in handy when he rushed me to the hospital the other week. It also comes in handy when we are, um, well... you know." I winked at Diane and she gave me the gagging with a finger gesture before we both burst into laughter.

"Ok, let's get this dress on you. Your man is waiting and my man is sitting out there being bored out of his mind. Why didn't we go with a bar again? Oh, that's right; David would have been drunk before the wedding began." Diane chortled and then we got to work getting my dress on me.

*　　*　　*　　*

I was standing there at the altar awaiting the arrival of my bride when I smelled something out of the ordinary. There was someone in the forest that hadn't been invited. It was a scent that I recognized and definitely one that I had hoped to never detect again.

I started scanning the tree-line for any inclination that this person was close by. I couldn't see him anywhere, but I knew he was there. I could feel his eyes boring a hole in my back.

I was startled from my thoughts when the music started playing. My attention was drawn to the back door of the cottage when the door opened and out stepped Diane. She was looking as lovely as ever in her rose colored satin dress. She stepped slowly with the beat of the music and came up the aisle toward me. When she made it to her spot, she looked up at me, winked, and smiled brightly.

Suddenly, the music changed and out stepped my betrothed. She looked more beautiful than I'd ever seen her. Her hair was curled and piled high upon her head. Her slender neck was so smooth and creamy that it made my mouth drool and my fangs extended, just a little, in anticipation of what was to come.

The cream-colored dress that she had chosen couldn't have been more perfect. The sleeves were off the shoulders, which emphasized that lovely neck even more. The bodice hugged her bosom tightly—enhancing the abundance that was already there—and then it flowed out just above the waistline, making for a floating sensation when she walked toward me.

It seemed to take an eternity for her to reach the altar where I was standing. I wanted to fly down and scoop her up into my arms, but I knew that she'd be pissed if I messed up this moment for her. I grinned at the thought of her temper taking over during a moment like this.

We caught each others' eye and smiled in unison. She looked so beautiful that I felt tears starting to well up in my eyes. The guests had all eyes on her. Camera flashes were exploding, but the only thing I saw was my beautiful bride.

Her slow ascent was finally coming to an end and she reached out her hand for me to help her step up onto the altar. I graciously accepted and lead her up to where we would declare our intentions to one another. When she stepped up beside me I could smell her perfume, but it was overpowered by the natural blood-scent that I loved so much.

As we stood there staring into each others' eyes, I couldn't help but to think of the creature hiding somewhere in this forest just watching what I was doing. He could see my beloved and would likely find a way to use my love for her against me. That's what he does when he wants something.

I was jolted out my unhappy thoughts by Fiona whispering, "Are you ready to do this? You'll be stuck with me forever." I smiled and replied, "The better to love you my dear." Then I bared my teeth just enough to make her snicker while attempting to retain her goddess-like composure.

I looked up at our officiator—Priestess Karenne—and nodded to signal that we were ready to begin the ceremony to bind our lives together for eternity. She nodded back and then we began.

"Welcome everyone! We have come together today to celebrate the binding of two lives. Alexander and Fiona have invited us all to witness their love and intentions to join as one being, under the watchful eyes of the Eternal Gods and Goddesses of Nature."

"Love is one thing that no being on earth can hold back. Love comes from within and no one can block its path to those that it has chosen. Love should only be given freely and never forced. Love is divine and should be treated as such."

Priestess Karenne paused, turned to Fiona, and then continued, "Fiona, is it true that you have come here tonight of your own free will?"

Fiona nodded fiercely and replied with a resounding, "Yes, I do!"

Priestess Karenne turned her attention to me and asked, "Alexander, is it true that you have come here tonight of your own free will?"

I didn't have to think for even a millisecond before blurting out, "I couldn't be any freer than I am tonight. Yes, I do!

The group of guests joined in with a quick chuckle and Fiona's smile couldn't have gotten any bigger than it already was.

With a smile on her lips, Priestess Karenne continued, "Please join hands with your betrothed and listen to that which I am about to say."

"Above you are the stars, below you are the stones, as time doth pass, remember..."

"Like the stones, your love should be firm and like the stars your love should be constant. Let the power of your love and the intellect of your mind guide you in your marriage, let the strength of your wills bind you together and the strength of your dedication make you inseparable."

34

The crowd was silent while the priestess spoke. Fiona's eyes were tearing up and I could feel the love surrounding us like the heat that emanates from her whole body. Unfortunately, I could also sense those uninvited eyes upon us.

Priestess Karenne continued, "Alexander, is it your wish to be joined with your betrothed, Fiona?"

"Yes, more than anything," I stated clearly.

"Fiona, is it your wish to be joined with your betrothed, Alexander?"

"It is my wish now and forever," Fiona said with a smile on her lovely face.

"Alexander, please take the ring and place it upon the third finger of Fiona's left hand."

I did just as she asked and kissed Fiona's hand lightly when the task was complete.

"Fiona, please take the ring and place it upon the third finger of Alexander's left hand." Fiona did as instructed.

"Please join hands and Alexander, repeat after me... I, Alexander, do take thee Fiona in the spirit of heaven and earth, with the love that is in my heart, as my chosen one and only love. I promise to love thee wholly and completely without restraint, in this life and beyond."

I repeated every word asked of me while clinging tightly to the hand of my bride. I found that the words had to be forced through the lump that was welling in my throat. Fiona had tears sliding down her face, but her expression was in a frozen state of happiness.

"Now Fiona, would you please repeat after me... I, Fiona, do take the Alexander in the spirit of heaven and earth, with the love that is in my heart, as my chosen one and only love. I promise to love thee wholly and completely without restraint, in this life and beyond."

Fiona repeated every word with love dripping from each syllable. As soon as she finished, I kissed her hands. I was so ready to be pronounced man and wife so that I could scoop her up into my arms.

"With that, and the power vested in me, I now pronounce you husband and wife. May your love be ever-lasting and lead you through life with the brightness of a guiding light. You may now kiss the bride!"

With those words spoken, I lifted Fiona into my arms and—with a background of cheers coming from the crowd—I kissed her with such force and passion that there wouldn't have been anyone who could have separated us. Fiona's arms were wrapped around my neck so tightly that it appeared she was afraid that letting go would cause her great distress.

I released her lips, let her slide back down to the floor, and looked deep into her eyes. She smiled up at me and, with the abruptness of a fog horn, her expression changed to shock. "What?" I asked.

Her smile reappeared and she said, "Isabella just woke up and is congratulating mommy and daddy." I placed my hand on her stomach and sure enough our little girl was bouncing around in there like she was so happy in her environment.

"HA, Isabella is wishing us well!" I shouted to the crowd. There was an uproar of laughter and a celebration that would last well into the night soon began.

We drank, ate, and were merry. Our guests ate their fill of the catered food and I had a slice of our wedding cake. It was delicious, and I probably would have eaten more of it had I still been alive. Fiona snacked around, but I could tell that these foods weren't what she was aching for. I would have to remedy that for her as soon as the opportunity presented itself.

Ahhh, we were married. I, Alexander Jenkins, had a wife and a child on the way. After all these years, I would have the life that I had desired for so many decades. I was happier than I'd ever been, but in the back of my mind I was worrying about our uninvited guest.

He had left as soon as the wedding was over, but if he's hanging around there will be trouble in the very near future. What that trouble would be, was yet to be seen. But I was certain that he wouldn't wait too long before declaring his intentions. I just hoped that he would wait until tonight was over.

Chapter 5

The wedding was over and all of the guests had gone home. I was completely exhausted and terribly famished. Alex had gone downstairs to, "get the honeymoon suite prepared" as he had stated, so I was sitting at the kitchen table having a cup of tea. I was still in my wedding dress and I was kind of reluctant to take it off and bring an end this glorious evening of love and celebration.

Diane had made sure that everything was cleaned up and that the photographer had gotten all of the pictures that he needed. She also made sure that he would have my photos ready for viewing in a few nights. She's been such a wonderful help during all of this and I wouldn't know what to do without her. Unfortunately, I had a bad feeling that she was going to be proven right with her concerns about mine and Isabella's safety.

During the entire ceremony, I had the feeling that someone was watching me. My werewolf sense of smell had been lessened since I was turned, but I knew that I had caught a whiff of something similar to the scent that Alex had when we first met. That meant there was another vampire in the forest while we were getting married— someone who was watching very intently and someone who made Alex nervous.

I could see the fear in his eyes mingling with the looks of love and happiness. I knew that he had sensed the other being, but I didn't mention it during our wedding. I wanted the wedding to be happy and cheerful and full of joy and love. Now that the wedding was over I couldn't smell or sense the presence of another vampire, so I decided to wait until tomorrow to mention it to Alex. I wanted my wedding night with the man I love; without distractions from other supernatural beings.

A few minutes later, Alex reappeared in nothing but his birthday suit. Ooohh, he is so sexy. A faint tingle began to creep its way up my body. The yearning for him began and the hunger I had been controlling all day would not be silenced.

"Are you ready for your wedding night, my beloved?" Alex asked while sliding slowly toward me.

I rose from my seat and nodded in affirmation. Before he could take another step I had rushed up to him. I can move very quickly when sex and feeding are involved—even in my mountainous condition.

Alex grinned and I could see his fangs begin their ascent. That sight in turn caused my longing to heighten and my own fangs made their appearance. This was going to be fun with a capital F!

Alex lifted me into his arms with the carefulness of a lioness carrying her cub. His fangs were fully extended now and mine weren't far behind. The lust for one another was too much to deny. Alex turned to head back toward the bedroom. His head tilted down toward mine and he kissed me fiercely. I returned the kiss just as urgently.

My arms went up around his neck and my fingers entangled with his hair. Alex turned his head slightly, just enough to bare his neck, and I took it. My fangs pierced his flesh with such force that it was like sticking a toothpick into softened butter.

Alex didn't even flinch. He just sped up his progression toward our honeymoon suite with such eagerness that we were there before I could take one gulp from his indolent blood flow. I released his neck as soon as I felt him placing me upon the bed.

He was floating above me. I looked around and he had placed red candles all around the room. I could smell the scent of wild flowers and he had hung a canopy of sheer fabric all around the bed. The room was gorgeous, but I was more interested in the naked man hovering above me.

"Come down here. I want you now..." I protested softly and reached my hands out to my husband.

Alex smiled and, instead of coming down to me, he grabbed me around the waist and pulled me up to him. Here we were, floating together in mid-air—me in my wedding dress and him buck naked.

40

His face went from happy to intense. I noticed the organ between his legs was starting to grow intensely. I knew what was coming and I was ready to take it; fully.

Alex grabbed a handful of my hair and gently pulled my head back to expose my neck. He went straight for that special spot that makes me squirm and he bit; hard. I gasped and he held me tighter with his other hand before lowering us down onto the bed.

He continued to feed while I was trying to remove my wedding dress. It had already served its purpose and all I wanted at that moment was to get out of it. I didn't care how, I just wanted out.

Alex released the ball of hair in his left hand and proceeded to start pulling at my dress right along with me. The dress just wasn't coming off. Alex stopped feeding and looked up at me with his blood-covered mouth. I grabbed his head with both hands and pulled his mouth down to mine.

While I was covering his face with kisses and licking the dripping blood from his lips, his hands continued to fumble with my dress until suddenly I heard a very loud ripping sound. I released his face and looked down to find that he had ripped the dress straight down the middle and my whole body was exposed.

I laughed out loud and wriggled my arms out of the sleeves as fast as I could. Alex was straddling me, making sure to be careful of our unborn child, waiting for me to finish. Once my arms were free we went straight back to one another like two magnets pulling towards each other.

"I love you so, my sweet. I can't believe that this day is finally here. We are now husband and wife and I can have you fully."

Alex's tone was a little frantic, like this was the last night we'd ever have together, and it made me somewhat nervous.

I backed away from him while getting up on my knees, motioned to my growing belly and, through stifled laughter, said, "Honey, I think you've already had me to the fullest."

Alex's brow wrinkled up and his head tilted to one side before he said, "You know what I mean, Mrs. Jenkins! Now come here and lets make the night last... at least until the sun comes up."

I giggled at the sound of my new name and then pressed my body against his. His hands tore at my bra straps and quickly had it removed. He turned my head and bite into the opposite side of my neck while I swooned from passion.

I wanted him inside me. I wanted all of him. I wanted to devour every last drop of blood he had. I wanted him to consume me, forever and always.

"Ooohhh you are so warm" he moaned. He loved the heat that emanated from my body, especially during our lovemaking. I hugged his cold body tighter. We were a perfect pair—him cool as ice and me as warm as fire.

"Take me, take me NOW!" I groaned. I couldn't take it any longer. My body was in an uproar. I'd fed and now I wanted MORE.

Alex laid me back down onto the bed; his hand ran down the side of my neck, down between my breasts, and then slowly circled each nipple with his thumb. Once his thumb had brought that small mound of flesh to life, his mouth followed. To prevent myself from forcing his whole body down on top of me, I was grabbing handfuls

42

I rushed downstairs to make sure that Alex hadn't slipped by me, and was actually waiting for me in bed. Once down there, I noticed that there were some things out of place. Alex is very meticulous about where things go, so I knew he hadn't just left things askew. My eyes darted from one corner of the room to another. I scanned every inch of our sanctuary from my standing point on the stairs.

Suddenly, my eyes settled upon something important—a lamp that was lying broken on the floor. I darted down the stairs and kneeled where the lamp was. It was Alex's favorite red lamp and it was shattered into a thousand little pieces.

This wasn't breakage from just accidentally knocking it over. This was like someone had picked it up and forcefully bashed it onto the floor. There were pieces radiating a few feet out.

I looked around, but no one was here. I sniffed the air and found the faint scent of my Alex. This was our bedroom after all, so his scent would be here. But, I went back to looking at the lamp and out of the corner of my eye I spotted something wet on the floor about three feet from where I was kneeling.

I crawled over to it; I swirled my finger in the dark, sticky goo, and then sniffed it. This was Alex's blood. I knew this hadn't been from our love-making because we had been on the bed the whole time and this was about six feet from the bed. Besides, we never waste a drop and certainly wouldn't have spread it around the room only to have to clean it up later.

I stood up, the room started to spin. Alex was gone. Someone had taken him. He would have never left me of his own free-will. He had been abducted by another vampire.

I screamed, "ALEX!!" and then the world went dark.

Chapter 6

"Fiona! Fiona, are you alright? Fiona, wake up!"

I felt someone tugging me up and yelling my name. When I finally opened my eyes, I saw a very blurry Samantha standing over me. Her face was full of concern and she was cradling me in her lap.

"I'm ok. Stop screaming, Sam. I'm alright." I was a little short with her, but this isn't how most people enjoy being awakened.

I sat up and looked around the room. Everything came flooding back. Alex was gone and someone had to have taken him against his will. I was all alone. The tears started flowing freely and Samantha looked very worried

"What is it Fiona? Are you ok? Is there any pain?" She was frantically feeling my forehead, checking my pulse, and feeling my stomach for contractions.

"Alex! Alex is missing!" I screamed in terror. "Alex has been taken by another vampire!"

"What? How do you know? Did someone hurt you? Did someone hurt Alex?" Samantha sounded as upset as I.

Through my sobs, I managed to tell her everything that had happened, including the fact that I had detected this scent during the wedding. "I should have told Alex about it. At least then he could have been prepared for what was about to happen."

"Fiona, I know that you are half werewolf and you have a fantastic sense of smell, but I can assure you that if you noticed the scent during the wedding, then so did Alex. He knew something was going to happen. That's why I'm here. He asked me to come over before dawn to check on you."

Her statement threw me for a loop. Alex had asked her to come over to check on me? He knew that something was going to happen and he hadn't mentioned it to me? Why would he do that? We are partners in all of this—what ever this was.

"What the hell do you mean he asked you to come over to check on me? Why the hell would he do that? What did he tell you... and WHEN did he tell you this?" I fired my questions at her so quickly that she never would have been able to answer them fast enough to satisfy my anger.

"Calm down Fiona. You blood pressure is dangerously high and your pulse is racing. Please, calm down and I will explain everything."

Suddenly, I had the most horrendous pain radiating throughout my stomach. The pain forced me back down onto the floor and I curled up in, what can only be described as, the fetal position. I was holding my stomach with both hands and the tears now falling were tears of physical pain instead of emotional turmoil. I heard Sam screaming at me to open my eyes and then everything went black for the second time in twenty-four hours.

When the world around me began to penetrate my senses once again, I was back in the hospital. Sam was hovering over me and one of her assistants was checking the machines that they had me hooked up to. I looked down at my own body and was grateful to see that I was still pregnant. I couldn't lose my husband and my daughter all in the same day.

"Welcome back," Sam said in her normally cheerful voice. "I'm glad to see you awake. Now if we could just keep you from doing that again we'd be doing well."

"What happened?" I asked with the strength of a frail, old woman.

"You wouldn't calm down, that's what happened. I told you that your blood pressure was sky high and your pulse was racing. The only thing your body could do was shut you down. You are a very stubborn woman, you know." Ah, Sam and her matter-of-fact statements.

"So the baby is alright? Isabella is ok?"

"Oh yes, your baby girl is perfectly fine. You were just having some nasty contractions because of your emotional state. Stress can bring on contractions in no time at all. I'm going to ask that you please try to stay calm. Your baby needs you to do that for her. Can you do that for your unborn daughter?" Sam looked at me with her *do as I say, young lady* expression—the kind of look that all children would see at some point in their lives. I know that I certainly had.

Of course I would do anything for my little angel, so I nodded and tried not to allow my eyes to release the tears that were immediately welling up. I bite my bottom lip, closed my eyes, and laid my head back on the pillow behind me.

"Good. Now let's see if we can figure out what's going on with Alex and then we'll see if we can get you out of here. Maybe you should call Diane and have her come to sit with you until you're discharged. It will be a few hours and, since the sun is up, you might as well just hang out here with us. You can't find Alex, or his abductor, when they should be somewhere sleeping."

She was right. I couldn't very well hunt down two vampires when they would be dead to the world, and besides, I had no idea where to start looking for a vampire that I didn't even know existed until last night.

"Alright, Sam, I'll hang out here for now and rest up. We'll make sure that Isabella really is alright. But, just know that as soon as dusk approaches I will be leaving this hospital... with or without your signature on those discharge papers."

Sam knew that I was serious. She nodded in agreement and then patted me on the hand before telling me, "Ok sweetie. We'll do it your way, but please stay in bed and stay calm during the day. I'll have the nurse bring you something to eat in a few minutes and then later we'll discuss your other nourishment requirements, as well as everything that has happened." Then she turned and left me in the capable hands of her assistant, without even waiting for an acknowledgement from me.

I knew exactly what Samantha meant by my "other nourishment requirements". She was talking about my need for blood—specifically my need for Alex's blood. I had never craved anyone else's blood except his. The more pregnant I became, the more my body demanded regular feedings from Alex. We all assumed it was because of the baby.

Ever since I became pregnant, this child has required her father to be close by—even more than a normal werewolf pregnancy would require. When I was having horrible morning sickness the only thing that would help was keeping Alex by my side. The closer he was to me, the better I felt. As the pregnancy progressed, Alex was able to be further from me without any adverse side effects.

Two weeks ago, I was able to be out all day in search of the perfect wedding dress while Alex was back in the cottage sleeping, without me feeling badly. But, that only lasts until the sun goes down. As soon as her daddy is awake, Baby Isabella is demanding nourishment and closeness from her father. I don't mind because Alex is always by my side when he is awake. He hates that he can't be with me twenty-four hours a day, but that's not even a possibility to consider.

As soon as the assistant had finished up her assessments, filled out her forms, and left, I picked up the bedside phone and dialed Diane's number. It was almost seven o'clock on a Sunday morning. She would probably be sleeping in with her husband and children. I hoped that I wouldn't be waking her, but I needed to tell her what was going on; I needed her by my side right now.

The phone rang once, twice, three times before I heard the click of someone picking up the phone on the other end. No one said anything, but I could tell that they were there. I was starting to worry when I finally heard Diane's voice in the background saying, "Give me the damn phone David." I snickered, and then Diane got on the line.

"Hello? This better be good." Diane was not a morning person.

"Hey, Diane, it's Fiona. I need you to come to the hospital, when you have time." I was calm, but the calmness in my voice didn't convey any meaning to Diane. Only the word *hospital* seemed to catch her attention.

"Hospital? Why are you in the hospital? Are you ok?" She questioned me.

"I'm ok, but there was an incident with high blood pressure, a racing pulse, contractions, and a missing husband. So could you come up here to Hopewell General and stay with me today? Sam has promised to release me by nightfall."

"A missing husband? What the hell are you talking about? Alex is missing?" Diane paused for just an instant and then said, "No, don't tell me. I will be up there in twenty minutes and then you can explain. Right now, just stay calm and I'm coming."

"Ok, I'll see you in..." Diane hung up before I could finish. I imagined that she was racing through her bedroom throwing out something to wear and washing her face as fast as she could. I'd seen her do it and it is quite the sight to see.

52

A few minutes later, a sweet little teenage girl dressed in a candy striper uniform came in with my breakfast—scrambled eggs, oatmeal, and two slices of whole wheat toast and strawberry jam. I was famished. I knew that I had until tonight before I would require sustenance in the form of blood. But for now, I was just stomach-growling hungry. So I ate my breakfast and waited for Diane to arrive.

Chapter 7

It was almost dawn and I knew that Fiona would have awakened to find me missing by now. I hoped that Samantha had made it to Fiona's side before something awful happened. We still didn't know the full extent of Fiona's powers, especially now that she was pregnant.

I was now the prisoner of Sebastian. He had come into the cottage and attacked me after drugging Fiona. She had been sleeping, so he just made sure she wouldn't be waking up for a few hours. I sensed him from within my dreams after Fiona and I had collapsed from our exciting escapade.

I awoke to find him standing over Fiona with a cloth over her mouth. I jumped over the bed at him, but he moved just enough that I landed on the floor. He picked up my favorite red lamp and launched it down upon me as hard as he could. It crashed down with the force of a cannonball being discharged during war. After that, I was out.

Now I'm here, in what can only be described as a dungeon. It was dark, moldy, wet, and it smelled like death. I was against a cold wall bound by my ankles and wrists with chains so heavy and thick that Zeus himself couldn't have broken them.

I was awake and wishing that I wasn't. At least in my dreams I could be with Fiona and our daughter without having to worry about someone like Sebastian. He was nothing but pure evil; the worst of the worst when it came to vampires. He was my creator and he had returned to see how his protégé was coming along.

I heard the door to the dungeon begin to open and I sensed that it was a vampire—only it wasn't Sebastian. The scent was familiar, but not exactly the way I remembered it. I didn't know who it was until she walked it. SERENA! Damn, anyone besides Serena!

"Well, well, well, fancy meeting you here, Alexander." She cackled with the laugh of a banshee. I instantly remembered why I had left her in life, and why I wanted nothing to do with her in death.

"Serena, what brings you to this lovely dungeon? Weren't you still alive the last time I saw you? When did you and your evilness align with Sebastian and his diabolism?" I sneered at the sight of her. She was such a bitch. How could I have ever thought I loved her?

"Ah, Alexander, don't be like that." She slithered up to me. She slid her hands up my chest until she grabbed my chin and jerked my head to the left. She sniffed up my neck and then right when I thought she was going to bite me, she pulled my mouth to her's and kissed me. I pulled my chin away from her hand and spit at her.

"I see that you haven't changed in death, Serena. You didn't answer my question... how is it that you've come to be with Sebastian? You do realize that he's an evil bastard, don't you?"

She walked away from me about three paces before turning back to me and answering. "Why of course I know all about Sebastian. He's the one who turned me all those years ago. It was about a year after he turned you. He had calmed his savagery and became a self-made gentleman."

She paused and gave me a look of disgust, "Something that you could never have done at such a young age. He was just a baby, but he saw the power he had over others and used that to his advantage."

I scoffed in disgust and refused to look at her. Sebastian was a beast, a savage, a demon from hell. Sebastian was Satan on earth. He had attacked me late one night, out in the middle of a corn field. He hadn't even given me a chance to run or even convince him that I didn't want to be this creature that I am.

He told me that he wanted an heir and he attacked. I remember feeling his own blood flowing down the back of my throat before hearing him say "Damn it! I killed another one!" Then he left me to die in that corn field.

Little did he know that I wasn't dead yet. I laid there in a pool of my own blood waiting for death to take me and just as I slid into darkness I remembered thinking that this was the end. I'd never have a life beyond being a farmer's son and working the fields. I'd never have the things I wanted. I'd never have the freedom that the savage fiend who'd done this to me had. Then, I was dead.

The next thing I knew, the sun was coming up. I opened my eyes and they felt like they would burn out of my skull. My whole body felt like it was overheating and would catch fire at any second. I was forced to my feet by the fear of the unknown. I ran for the tree line and reached a cave that I'd played in as a child. I slept there that day and then the next night began my life as a vampire.

"You know that Sebastian was the best thing that could have happened to you. You were nothing, with no potential. Now look at you. You have a fortune, a home of your own, freedom, and even nice clothes. You've definitely improved since we last spoke." She smiled her Cheshire cat grin. I use to think that her smile was lovely until I discovered the ugliness beneath it.

"Lest you forget, I also have a wife and child on the way. Something you could never have given me." Serena had been sterile even before she had been turned by the bastard Sebastian. If I had married her all those years ago, we wouldn't have had any children.

"Oh Alexander, must you be so cruel? I've seen your bitch. How could someone like that even appeal to you? How can I say this nicely? She's a little bigger than the girls of our time. If you know what I mean." Serena smirked at her self-presumed slyness.

"If you'll recall, I preferred the girls with curves. It was always like hugging a stick when I was with you. I'm glad that we never had sex or I might have injured you."

Serena's face was covered in shock, anger, and complete disbelief that I had made such a statement. She didn't even reply, she just turned and stomped right out the door—slamming it behind her.

I heard her speaking to someone outside the door. "He's nothing but an insolent jackass. I don't know why you wanted to bring him here. He'll bring nothing but aggravation to both of us. Just kill him now and get it over with."

As soon as I heard the other person, I knew it was Sebastian. "Be calm, Serena. I have my reasons; you will sit by and tolerate him if you know what's good for you."

My skin was crawling from the fear and total disgust of coming face-to-face with my creator. It had been more than fifty years since we'd last crossed paths and that didn't end any better than when I was murdered by his hand seventy years prior. I thought we had said all that was to be said those many years ago. Why would he want me now?

The door opened again and in stepped Sebastian. He looked exactly the same as he had during our last visit. He was tall, around six and a half feet, and he had a head full of long black hair. His hair was so dark that it reminded me of an onyx. His eyes were almost as dark as his hair. There was no true color in the irises of those orbs—only blackness.

Sebastian wasn't a muscular creature. He wasn't nearly as well-built as I was. He hadn't been a farmer's son when he was turned. Sebastian had been a banker all those years ago. He sat behind a desk, filled out forms, and counted his money while trying to find more ways to weasel even more money from unsuspecting common folk. Because of that, he had a scrawny, wiry frame. But, don't let his looks fool you, he could still hold his own in a bar fight if need be; without using fangs.

58

"Hello Alexander, my son" he cooed. His coolness made a shiver run up my spine. "It has been far too long since our last visit. What have you been doing with yourself these days?"

"Sebastian, why ask such irrelevant questions? You know damn well what I've been doing with myself, as you've been spending time spying on me. I hope you enjoyed the wedding ceremony last night." I tried to keep my voice calm and steady. It always pissed him off when I wouldn't react to him, no matter how unsettled I was in his presence.

"Ah yes, I did happen to stop by and take in the show last night. It was very entertaining. The concept of you taking a bride is quite humorous. I never saw you as a marrying man and here I see that you even have a ring to show for it."

He came over, grasped my left hand, and spun my wedding ring around on the finger. He was only inches from my face and I could feel his breath on my ear while he was inspecting my token of affection from Fiona. I could smell Serena all over him and memories of my time with her flashed before my eyes. God, I hated her.

Sebastian stopped playing with my ring. He slid his hand down my arm, down my side, and then up over my chest. He ran one finger up my neck, circling the lump in my throat before continuing up to my lips. His thumb took the place of his finger and he slid it across my lips while licking his own.

Did I mention that he liked it both ways? Members of both sexes had been playmates in Sebastian's bed. He hated that I had never shown any interest in his wiles.

"Ah Alexander, you haven't changed a bit. You are still as sexy as you were all those years ago. Why is it that you never made it into my bed? Oh yes, you only like girls—disgusting little creatures, with all of that soft flesh and moodiness. How can you enjoy such things when you could have this?" He motioned to his own body and I felt my stomach professing its own objections to such considerations.

"Oh please, don't even attempt to disguise your disgust for my sake!" Sebastian yelled. He walked away from me and started for the door.

"Wait! Why have you brought me here? What are your intentions? I demand to know!" I screamed my inquiries at him.

Sebastian slowly turned and, before I realized it, he flew straight at me and was standing with his nose no more than an inch from mine. "You will find out when I want you to know. You will be my prisoner until I decide otherwise. You will stay right here in this chamber until I feel like releasing you... if I decide to release you."

Before I could voice my protest, Sebastian forced his lips onto mine. His tongue forced my lips to part and he was kissing me with such commanding that I couldn't stop him. I only had one weapon at my disposal to stop his oral rape; my fangs. I bite down on his tongue as hard as I could. My fangs pierced the tender flesh and even when he tried to get away I hung on solidly.

Sebastian was squealing like a stick pig during slaughtering season. He stumbled away from me and his tongue tore in the process. His mouth was bleeding profusely and the scent penetrated my nostrils. I could feel my hunger rising to the surface. Even though I had fed from Fiona just a few hours earlier, the scent and sight of fresh blood was something that no vampire could resist.

"DAMN YOU, ALEXANDER! YOU WILL PAY FOR THIS, YOU BASTARD CHILD OF MINE!"

Sebastian was pissed. He came rushing back up to me and—with as much strength as he could muster—he belted me right in the stomach. I slumped over and started coughing up blood. My hands were still constrained by the chains so I couldn't even protect my injury.

Sebastian reared back his fist and belted me again, right in the same spot. This time I heard a few ribs crack and I felt one puncture the left lobe of my lungs. I was coughing so violently that I couldn't think straight.

My arms were stretched to their limits and I considered breaking my hands to get out of the shackles. But, if I did so, I wouldn't stand a chance against Sebastian in his current state of animosity. The pain was enough to force me to be still and just hope that the two punches were enough to satisfy Sebastian's rage.

"You will NOT leave here! I have plans for you and you will fulfill them! I am your sire and you will OBEY ME!" He spat these words at me like he was trying to convince me that my life was over, but deep down he knew that I would never obey him.

I coughed and managed to catch my breath just long enough to sputter, "You know that will never happen, Sebastian. I hate you and you will die at MY hand."

Sebastian rushed back up to me, grabbed my hair and pulled my head up so that our eyes met. "You will obey or your new bitch will be the next on my list of conquests. I'll make sure that she screams your name before I take her. Then your child will be born unto me and I'll be sure to take really good care of her until she is old enough to be my slave...", he hissed at me.

I growled and tried to get loose. I snapped at him, but he backed far enough away so that I couldn't clamp down on anymore of his tender flesh. I would kill him. He would never lay a finger on Fiona, and my Isabella would never know the likes of him if I could help it.

I could feel the sun rising. I would have to sleep soon. I wished that I had more time to think things over, but once the sun comes up I'll be out—whether I want to or not. I fell to sleep thinking of Fiona and hoping that she was safe and sound with Samantha. I would see her again very soon... one way or another.

Chapter 8

The sun had come up and I was waiting on Diane to arrive at my bedside. I had eaten the breakfast that Sam's assistant brought to me and was now sipping on a warm cup of herbal tea. I heard a knock at the door and assumed it was Diane. In walked Sam.

"Wow, back so soon?" I asked. "Did you miss the company of the hormonal, pregnant woman who has been abandoned by her newlywed husband?"

Diane gave me a look of discontent before looking down at the chart in her hands. Her eyes glanced up at me, but quickly darted back down to the chicken scratch that she called handwriting. She walked slowly toward the bed, stopping to check the machine readings along the way. She was starting to worry me.

"What? Why do you look so freaked out, Sam? You know I hate it when people do that!" I really do hate it when people do that. It causes me to freak out right along with them before I even know what we're freaking out about.

Sam sat down beside me on the hospital bed, placed her hand over mine, and began with, "Ok, Fiona, I don't want you to worry..."

"Oh yes, like that's not how people announce bad news." I rolled my eyes and braced myself for the worst.

"No, it's not really all that bad. It's more unsuspecting news, rather than bad news."

"Like that makes me feel any better..."

"Fiona, you know how we've discussed the unknowing gestational period of your pregnancy? How a human gestation generally last forty weeks, and a werewolf gestation generally runs around thirty weeks?"

"Yes, yes, I know all of this. And you said that we would just watch the baby's development and see how it goes. According to the last scan you said she was right on with human development and that we shouldn't expect her arrival until close to August. Right?"

"Well, yes, but it was still a wait and see for all of us since this pregnancy is the first of its kind."

"Alright, damn it! Just spit it out Samantha! What the hell is wrong with the baby?"

A machine to my left started beeping and Sam jumped up off the bed to check it. "Calm down Fiona, your pulse is accelerating again. We don't want another episode like this morning."

I took a deep breath and closed my eyes while lying back on the pillow. I would not get all worked up again. So what if I was alone, pregnant, and was now finding out that something was wrong. I had to calm down.

"Ok, I'm sorry Sam. You know how I hate this, so just tell me. Tell me quickly, like ripping off a bandage, quick and painless." I took another deep breath and awaited the bad news.

"Fiona, stop being so dramatic, it's not that bad. I just wanted to tell you that the new scans indicated that your baby is growing at a much faster rate than she was previously. It looks like she will be reaching full growth in a matter of weeks instead of months. Instead of an August birth, we're looking at a May birth."

A wave of relief, combined with total shock, washed over me with the force of a transfer truck. I was ever so grateful that Alex's daughter was alright, but we weren't ready for her arrival yet. We didn't even have a nursery ready yet. I hadn't even begun to buy baby clothes. We'd been too busy planning the wedding and... I thought I had more time!

"What? What do you mean weeks? How can this be? You said August. But, we aren't ready. I'm not ready! Where is Alex? How can I be here, alone? I can't do this without him. He wanted to be a father so badly. Where is Alex?"

I could feel the air escaping my lungs. I wasn't ready for this. I started to scramble out of the bed. I had to find Alex. I started pulling wires off of my body, out of my veins, and from around my waist. I couldn't stay in this bed for one more minute.

"Fiona! What are you doing? Lay back down! You can't go anywhere right now!" Sam was trying her damnedest to hold me back, but I'm a vampirized werewolf, and much stronger than her.

"NO! I have to find Alex! I have to find him now! He has to be here when his baby is born! I can't do this alone!" I was frantic to get out of there. I was opening and closing drawers, just trying to find my clothes. Even in this state of mind, I knew that I wasn't leaving without my clothes.

"Where the FUCK are my clothes?" I screamed at Sam.

Sam was rushing around the room following me from one location to the other. She wasn't offering any help in my search. For all I knew, she'd burned the damn things and was now secretly laughing at me during my gratuitous search.

Sam grabbed me by both shoulders and spun me around to face her. I was surprised at her forcefulness, but it brought me out of my frenzy. She looked me right in the eyes and said in a slow, calculating tone, "Fiona, stop. You are not helping anyone by doing this. You can not help Alex at the risk of harming yourself or your child. Would he want you coming after him? I'm sure he's mentioned something about that in your months together."

I looked at her with bewilderment. "About not coming after him if he goes missing?" I asked. She nodded. I thought for a moment and seemed to recall him mentioning something to that extent in passing. I remembered dismissing it as him being paranoid and not thinking anything else about it.

"Do you think he knew something like this would happen? But, how could he? If he was expecting something like this to happen..." I was having a light bulb moment here. If Alex was expecting someone to come after him, then that meant he knew WHO would be coming after him!

I grabbed Samantha's arms and demanded to know who. "Sam, tell me! Tell me now! WHO was Alex expecting to come after him? You've known him much longer than I have, so you should know who would do this."

"Fiona, if you will calm down and get back into bed I will happily tell you everything I know. Please?" I agreed and Sam led me back to bed. She spent a good ten excruciating minutes hooking me back up to all of the monitors and making sure all of the machinery was working correctly. She checked my blood pressure, pulse, eyes, ears, breathing—anything she could think of to torment me even further.

When she finally finished with every mundane task she could come up with, she sat down on the end of the bed, folded her legs under her, laid her hands in her lap, and looked knowingly at me. I could have screamed, but I stayed calm so that she would tell me what I wanted to know. I sat there quietly waiting for her to begin, but when she didn't I growled my unhappiness at her.

"Ok, ok. Don't start getting all huffy again. What exactly would you like to know?" she asked.

"I want to know who has Alex and why, and I want to know NOW. No more beating around the bush. Get straight to the point or I will be up and out of this hospital before you can even attempt to call security."

She knew I was serious so she didn't even attempt to work up to the answers. She simply blurted out, "His creator, Sebastian, has him. Most likely because he hates how humanized Alexander has become."

"What do you mean 'humanized'? He's a vampire. How can he be 'humanized'?"

"Well, he's not out there killing and raping everyone in town, is he?"

"Of course not! He says he hasn't done that in a very long time. But what difference does that make to another vampire?"

"Well, his creator was a savage beast who cared nothing about anyone. All he wanted was to murder, rape, and feed. He liked killing people and would even do it without feeding on them. He just enjoyed death and defeat of the weaker humans around him."

Sam stopped to let that soak in. When I didn't say anything she continued with her story. I could only hope that this wouldn't take long.

"From what Alexander has told me, Sebastian thought he had actually killed Alex the night he turned him. Sebastian was a young vampire and he wanted to make others like him. Most vampires are turned after much consideration, therefore when it is done they have older, wiser vamps there to lead them through their changes and to help keep their young cravings in check.

Sebastian didn't have that. He had killed his creator as soon as he turned. Leaving Sebastian to learn the ropes of vampirism all alone and to, ultimately, decide how he wanted to spend his own eternity."

"Anyway, when Sebastian found out that he had successfully changed Alexander, all he wanted was for Alexander to be the same kind of savage killer he was. When he discovered that Alexander was actually following the laws of traditional vampire covenants, he was furious and vowed that he would bring Alexander over to his side—one way or another."

"I suspect that Sebastian heard wind of you marriage and upcoming birth. Something miraculous like that won't be kept a secret for long." Sam looked thoughtful and began to get off track.

"Vampires from far and wide will soon start making their way to see the vampire and werewolf offspring. The female werewolf population may actually be in danger of being taken by male vampires looking to be reborn as new men, like Alexander. Not to mention what the vampire females will try to do to the male werewolf population."

"Ok Sam, back to the real reason we're discussing this... Alex!"

"Oh, sorry. So, years ago when Alexander and I first became, um, friends, he had told me that if he ever went missing to not come looking for him. He said that he would find a way back to me, but he didn't want me to put myself in danger looking for him."

"Apparently, this happens every so many decades. Sebastian will come back looking to reap his revenge on Alexander's insolence and Alexander always finds a way to get away from him. Luckily, I never had to worry about that... until now, of course."

"So what am I suppose to do? I can't just sit by and wait for him to find a way to get away from this madman. We have a child on the way—apparently pretty damn soon. What if this time Alex can't get away from Sebastian? What if Sebastian has tired of this routine and finally kills Alex? I can't do this alone. I can't lose my husband after everything we've been through. I just can't!"

The tears started to flow freely down my face. Sam crawled up beside me in the bed and hugged me tightly. She had become such a great friend in the last few months. I always felt ashamed that I had thought she was a man-stealing bitch in the beginning and here she was trying to comfort me in my moment of despair.

I was sobbing heavily and Sam was just letting me cry. There was nothing that she could have said that would have made me feel any better about this situation anyway. I heard a knock at the door and in walked Diane.

"Ok I'm here." When she realized the state that I was in and her eyes shot from me to Sam and back again. "Oh God, is he dead?"

Chapter 9

The sun must have gone down, because I awoke in the same dungeon that I fell asleep in. I was still chained by my ankles and wrists to the cold, wet wall of this cell. I noticed that my ribs had healed during the daylight hours and I felt pretty rejuvenated. My ankles and wrists were sore and raw from the constant friction between flesh and metal. I hated to think about it, but I knew that I would have to break a few bones to get myself loose from my binds.

Sebastian was probably too busy feeding and enjoying Serena's corruption to come straight to me when he awoke. So, I probably had some time to get out of here before worrying about running into him. Or at least I hoped so.

I looked up at my hands and then down at my feet. I wondered which would be easier to release without falling flat on my face. I reckoned that my hands would have to be the first victims, especially since it would be easier to work with them than with broken feet.

I started pulling and twisting my left hand. I could feel the skin burning from the pressure. I twisted a little harder. Finally I felt my knuckles start to crack. The pain was intense, but I've felt worse. I kept pulling. My knuckles soon broke into several small pieces and my flesh was being torn from my hand. With one last loud pop, I was finally able to slide my fingers out and into freedom.

My hand was all mangled and twisted out of what would be considered a normal shape. I held it up in front of my face so that I could focus on popping bones back into place. When a vampire isn't sleeping an injury away, it is quite painful to repair it. You have to focus all your strength into this one spot and hope that you have fed recent enough to heal quickly. The further you are from your last feeding, the longer it will take to heal.

The hand just hung there like a limp piece of dead animal flesh. I focused all of my energy right into the center of my palm. I could feel the shards of bone sliding toward their intended locations. The pain of reuniting the broken fragments was just as brutal as when they had been torn apart. I groaned from the discomfort, but knew that this was the only way to escape my prison.

Finally my hand was back in the condition it was suppose to be. I wasn't sure if I'd have the energy to do it with the other one though. I needed to feed. I needed my Fiona! I used my now healed hand to pull and yank at the chain holding my right hand hostage. I would have to find a way to break the chains instead of subjecting myself to another broken appendage.

I couldn't get the chain to break. I yanked, jerked, and twisted the chain with all my might, but it only stretched the links a small amount; not nearly enough to break them. Just then the door burst open and there stood Sebastian.

The instant that he saw what I had been doing, he flew up to me and slapped me across the face with such force that the opposite side of my head hit the wall behind me. I was rattled for a moment and everything was fuzzy, but I shook it off. I bared my teeth at him and then struck him in the throat with my one free hand.

Sebastian was coughing and sputtering from the blow while I was trying my damnedest to get the other hand free from the shackles. Sebastian recovered and came at me. I timed it just right, and slugged him in the face just as he made it within reach. He had been coming at me so quickly that I didn't even have to put much force into the punch. He went flying back across the room and landed on his back.

I struggled to get myself free. I felt my right hand starting to crack from the pressure, but there was no other way to get out of these chains. I would just have to fight with my left until the right healed.

Sebastian was starting to climb up off the floor. My hand was halfway through the shackles. Sebastian rose to his feet, looked in my direction, and then flew straight for me. I yanked one good time and my hand broke the rest of the way and went flying out of the shackles.

Sebastian came up on me so quickly that if you'd blinked you would have missed it. He grabbed my broken and tattered hand and squeezed with all his might. I screamed at the top of my lungs and nearly passed out.

"You. Will. Die!" Sebastian yelled into my face.

"Not if I can help it, you bastard!" I screamed back.

Sebastian squeezed my hand even harder and I crumpled down to my knees from the pain. Sebastian kneeled down slowly. He grabbed my hair with his other hand and pulled my head up so quickly that I was surprised my neck didn't snap.

"You are a disgusting excuse for a vampire, Alexander. I am literally sickened by your..." he gagged a little when he continued, "humanity."

I couldn't move because of the pain, but in a low whispered voice I managed to get three little words out, "You're just jealous."

"JEALOUS? Are you serious?" Sebastian scoffed. "I could never be jealous by such a miserable creature. You renounce your own kind for the stench of a simple forest creature! Why would I ever be jealous of the likes of you?"

Sebastian was fed up with me. He threw my mangled hand to the floor and then started pacing the room. I was still chained to the wall by my ankles, but at least my hands were free now. I just had to keep him occupied long enough to allow my hand to heal.

"Yes, jealous! You know that I have something you'll never have... someone who loves me!"

That drew his attention. Sebastian turned around so quickly that I could feel the wind from his body. His looked unsettled and confused that I would even say such a thing.

"You think I want such a thing? Do you really think that YOU want such a thing? You are no true vampire. You are some human wannabe. You sicken me with you thoughts of love, family, happiness... you have a child on the way! That's not even possible! The consideration of such an abomination makes me want to tear your head off of your shoulders right now. "

I straightened my body up—the pain in my hand was starting to ease—and continued this conversation while Sebastian paced the room in complete bewilderment that I would suggest such things of him.

"Yes, I do believe that you want such things. Why else would you collect people like a dog collects bones? Why else would you have a bitch like Serena around you? Why else would you continue to come after me decade after decade? You want..." I paused. "No, you NEED someone to love you, want you, and to desire your affections."

Sebastian walked back over and stood directly in front of me. In my heightened hunger and frustration, I could smell his blood. I was so hungry. I needed blood. Just a little closer and I could get him. If only this hand would hurry and heal so I could use it. Damn it!

"Ah, are you hungry, Alexander? I'd be more than happy to feed you, if you would relinquish this ridiculous idea that you need love and a family. Just come back to me and I will retrain you in the true vampire ways. I will teach you how to be ruthless and to take what you want, instead of what you are offered. We are vampires; we don't have to ask for anything. We just take what we want!"

Sebastian roared to the room around us. He was reveling in his immortality and thoroughly enjoying it. He lifted his fists to the ceiling and shouted, "WE ARE GODS!!"

"We are not gods! You're a diabolical demon from Hell! I would never forsake my beloved and our child! Especially not for the likes of you! You know that real vampires don't live the way you and your followers do! Unlatch these damn chains and I'll show you the strength of a real vampire!" My blood-lust was growing by the minute. I just wanted him to come close enough for me to grab him.

Sebastian began to pace the floors right in front of me—he always did that when he needed to think. He would run his hands through his hair, fiddle with the rings on his fingers, and then he would turn to pace in the opposite direction. He didn't say a word for about five minutes, but I just wanted to devour every drop of his blood. I would take from him what he took from me all those years ago. I would kill him!

"Alexander, I just don't understand the hold this female has over you. What kind of power does she have that makes you want to give up your vampire ways? Why would you ever choose to only feed from one person, when there are millions of worthless humans out there for us to enjoy?"

He walked up to me—almost within reach—his face was pleading for me to understand his viewpoint on this subject. "My son, how can you deny that we are vicious, blood-loving beasts of the night? You can't! This is what we were created for. If there is a god, He created us to live off of the blood of these barbaric humans. You are wasting your God-given talents by shutting yourself up in a little house in the forest."

"Come with me. Be with Serena and me. We'll refresh your memory on how good it feels to be a fiendish creature of the night.

Don't you remember how much fun it was in those early days? Flying through the night sky, knowing you had the power to take the life from any one of those pests below you. Picking and choosing one or two of the females to rape and torture before draining her dry; hearing those screams of terror stop abruptly when you break their necks."

He stepped just close enough for me to grab his arm. I spun him around and wrapped my arms around him. His back was against me and he was squirming to get loose. "LET ME GO! I WILL KILL YOU IF YOU DON'T LET ME GO NOW!"

"No, Sebastian. This will be the end of you. I will be sure to finish off Serena too, when I'm through with you." With that I bite deep and hard into his neck. I tore into the flesh as roughly as I could. I wanted to make sure that he was not spared any of the pain that I could inflict on him at this time.

He screamed and wriggled in my arms. I would not let go. I was hungry and I would feed! He roared louder than any creature I'd heard before. His blood was cool, sluggish, salty, and thick. I hadn't had blood from another vampire in almost thirty years. I had forgotten how thick it was.

Suddenly, the door opened and I was distracted just enough for Sebastian to tear away from me and spin around to attack. He tore into me with all the power at his disposal. He was punching, scratching, biting, and kicking. I couldn't get away from him.

I tried to fight back, but he was worse than a wild animal cornered in a cage. He bellowed that he would kill me and then he would kill my wife and daughter. He shouted that he would make sure that everyone I knew and loved would die a slow, painful death at his hand.

He had finally gotten me down on the floor and was kicking and screaming. He jumped on top of me and started biting me. I could feel his fangs tearing at my flesh like a savage dog that had just caught a rabbit for his dinner. But, Sebastian wasn't biting me to feed, he was biting me to tear me apart piece by piece.

I tried to turn over so that I could get into a better position to fight back, but he kept knocking me back down. I was face down on the floor with this bastard on my back. I could feel my body being torn apart and even heard a few bones in my back snapping. My body was starting to go numb and I could feel the room spinning. My whole body went limp and I was thinking that this was the end and I would never see my beloved wife again or meet our little daughter.

In those last moments, I remember wondering who it had been that opened the chamber door and distracted me enough to lose my grip on Sebastian. I heard Sebastian asking someone how they had gotten in here. I vaguely detected a flash of light out of my right eye (the left had been smashed during Sebastian's attack). Then, I heard screams and Sebastian shouting for help. Lastly, I sensed a large explosion of heat before I passed out.

Chapter 10

It was nearly nightfall. Sam had gone to the lab to do some work and promised that she would return before it was time for me to leave. I hadn't had anymore problems with blood pressure or increased pulse ever since Diane arrived. She had gone straight to work on cheering me up and helping me prepare a plan of attack in order to get my husband back.

Before she'd gone to the lab, I'd made Sam tell me Sebastian's full name—it's Sebastian Lance, if you're curious—and then I sent Diane to the library to look up everything she could find about this man from the past. It turns out that he was only a few years older than Alex in his human age and he had been turned into a vampire only a few weeks before Alex (there was a newspaper article that mentioned that he'd gone missing). He had been a greedy and ruthless man in life, and it appeared that he was just as greedy and ruthless in death.

Diane found a few property holdings under his name in a neighboring town. One was an empty, abandoned warehouse, there were a few apartment buildings, and some vacant lots. Apparently all old vampires have a decent amount of property. How else would they be able to survive in this money-hungry culture?

I told Diane that I highly doubted Sebastian would be holding Alex in an apartment building or on a vacant lot. So, that left the abandoned warehouse for us to check out. The warehouse would have lots of places to hide someone, without anyone hearing them scream in the middle of the night. There would be lots of places where the sun wouldn't shine on those who didn't want to be burnt to a crisp. I just hoped that Alex was still alive.

I was growing impatient with Sam's slowness. She had promised to return forty-five minutes ago so that we could discuss a few things before I left. I had warned her that I would leave with or without her permission, but secretly I really wanted her to understand and condone my leaving the hospital.

Just then Diane walked back in from a coffee run. "Whew! You'd think it was feeding hour at the zoo with all the people crowded into the cafeteria downstairs."

Diane has never been one for subtlety. After taking a sip of her coffee and holding it out to me in offering—I declined, of course— she asked, "So, has Sam made it back? When are we getting out of here and finding that man of your's?"

"Huh? You don't think you're coming with me do you?" I couldn't believe that she would even suggest putting herself in such danger.

80

"Hell yes I'm going! You're not going out there alone, in your condition. I will be accompanying you to the dance, Ms. Fiona." She bowed and giggled like a madwoman. I couldn't help feeling grateful for such a wonderful friend, but I couldn't let her do this.

"Diane, you have a family and children to think about. I can't be responsible for something happening to you and leaving your children mother-less and your husband a widower. I just can't allow it."

"Since when have I ever let you allow anything? You're kidding yourself if you think I'm going to let my best friend—pregnant friend at that—go out and battle a deadly, revenge-seeking vampire on her own. And don't give me any of that bull about you being able to take care of yourself and all about the new, special powers you have. Hell, you've only used the fire thingy the one time, so you don't even know if it still works."

I started to speak, but Diane held up her hand for me to stop. "Don't even start, Fiona. This is NOT a discussion. I will be going with you or I'll have Sam come in here with a sedative and handcuffs to keep your stubborn ass in that damn hospital bed!"

I could tell that Diane was fed up with me. She only cusses like a sailor when she's highly passionate about something. I knew that she would do what she said and that I wouldn't get out of this without taking her along. So I nodded and said, "Ok, ok. Calm down. You can go..."

"Damn right I can go! I wasn't asking!"

"... IF you stay back and don't get into the battle unless absolutely necessary."

"Ok, that's fine. I don't wanna become vampire dinner anyway."

"AND, if something happens to me you have to promise to run. Run as fast as you can and as far as you can, until you KNOW that no one is coming after you. Do you promise?"

Diane nodded her head vigorously and replied, "Of course! Running as fast as I can away from a monster isn't something that you have to tell me to do." She smiled and winked at me. Diane was the only person I knew who could make me laugh in the most dire of situations.

"Ok, now that that's settled. Look what I've got." She picked up what looked like a stack of papers. She opened up the paper and spread it out on the foot of the bed.   It was a map of the area where Sebastian's warehouse was located.

"Ah, Diane! That's great!" I sat up straight on the bed and folded me legs under me until I was on my knees looking over every square inch of that map.

"Yep, I found it downstairs in the lobby. It's funny the things you can find in a hospital. Anyway, look right here..." Diane was pointing to a spot in the center of the map. She had drawn a big red circle around a place called the *International Warehouse District of Samson*.

"So is this where it's at?" I asked. She nodded and I started calculating how long it would take us to get there.

"Don't bother; I've already deduced that it will take up approximately fifty minutes to get there and then another five to find the right warehouse. So..."

Diane looked at her watch and then glanced out the window. "It will be around eight-thirty when we get there. We'll have about fifteen minutes of daylight left when we arrive, so we'll have to move quickly and hope that we can come upon Alex before the sun goes down and Sebastian awakes."

I got up off the bed and started removing all of the wires that were attached to me. I'd already given Sam enough time to get back in here and release me; I couldn't afford to wait any longer. This had to be timed just right so that we could find Alex before the vamps awoke, and still be able to get him out of there as soon as the sun went down. I couldn't be waiting around in this damn hospital.

"What are you doing? Shouldn't you wait until Sam comes in here and does all of that?" Diane asked tentatively.

"I'm getting ready to go. I've given Sam all the time I can afford to give her. I warned her this morning that I would leave when the time came, whether she had signed me out or not. So, I'm leaving. Now help me find my shoes, please."

Diane roamed around the room looking under the bed, under the tables, and finally found my shoes shoved into the back of a storage closet—along with a bag that had my clothes in it (I hadn't found those earlier). I stripped off the ugly blue and white striped hospital gown—it's not like it was covering anything anyway—and proceeded to pull my clothes out of the plastic bag. I slipped on my pants and started to pull my top over my head when I got a sudden jolt of electricity run through my stomach.

I grabbed my stomach with both hands and steadied myself. I looked down at the location of my unborn baby and noticed that my stomach was glowing. It reminded me of when my hands were glowing all those months ago and I ended up killing the whole werewolf council. I could feel heat radiating from my womb. At that moment, I realized that my power wasn't actually my power. It was Isabella's power!

"WHOA! What the hell is that?" Diane shouted while pointing at my stomach. "Are you ok? Do you want me to get a nurse or something?"

"No, a nurse can't help. Remember me telling you about my fire hands?" She nodded. "Well, apparently it wasn't from me." I pointed below.

"You mean..."

"Yeah, it looks like Isabella is the one with the powers."
Just then, Sam walked in. "Well, it looks like it's... oh my God!"

Chapter 11

Samantha came running over to me and placed both hands on my bare stomach. She jerked her hands away almost as soon as they touched me. "OUCH! Oh my god, Fiona! You're burning up. I need to get you back on these monitors right now!"

I jumped back from her, "NO! I will not stay here to be poked and prodded while Alex could be out there dying. I am in no harm from this, and neither is Isabella. This is HER doing, not mine. We are so hungry..." I felt my fangs descending into my mouth.

The hunger was starting to claw its way to the surface the closer it got to being nightfall. Alex would be waking soon and it had been almost twenty-four hours since our last feeding. I needed his blood; I needed it immediately!

Sam came closer, and in hushed tones said, "It's ok, Fiona. I know that you're hungry and I know that you miss Alex. Can we at least take a look at Isabella before you leave?" I took a moment to regain my composure, but Sam took my silence as indecision. "Please? It will only take a minute or two."

She was holding her hands up like she was ready to block me if need be. Diane was staying over in a corner of the room, just watching all the commotion and waiting for me to decide when I was ready to leave. She knew better than to get in my way; I had already warned her about the power of a vampire's blood lust.

Finally I decided to allow Sam to do an ultrasound, "Yes, we will take a look, but Sam, this better be quick because the hunger is starting to take over. Isabella needs her father's blood and she needs it soon."

"Ok, stay calm. I'm just going to step right outside the door and grab the machine. Stay right here." She started walking toward the door and would turn around and look at me every two steps. "It's just right outside the door." She pointed at the door like I was some crazed imbecile.

"Damn it, Sam! Just get the stupid thing already. I'm not some damn dog that needs to be trained on how to stay." She was starting to piss me off.

She walked out into the hallway and immediately returned pushing the ultrasound machine in front of her. She asked me to lie on the bed; I complied. Sam plugged the machine in, and then got it all booted up and ready to go. Since I didn't have anything but a bra and pants on, I didn't have to worry about pulling my shirt up, as my globe of a stomach was already fully in view.

Diane came to the other side of the bed and held my hand. Sam squirted a giant dollop of that gel they use for ultrasounds and spread it all over my stomach. But, it quickly started sizzling like bacon in a skillet. She put another pile of the goopy mess on just to make sure we had enough. Then, we all took a deep breath and looked at the flickering screen.

There she was, my baby girl. She was the miracle child between a vampire and his werewolf/vampire bride. She was the child who should never exist, and yet had always been wanted.

The baby was a hot, bright, white color. My stomach was glowing red, but the baby was a pure, intense white. She was moving around as frantically as a tadpole seeking to escape a rain-filled mud puddle.

"Well, aside from the glowing, she looks like a happy and healthy fetus. She's moving perfectly. All of her organs look great. Her heartbeat looks stable. All in all, she looks fantastic."

"But? I can hear a *but* in your voice."

"Well, you remember that this morning I told you that she was growing faster?"

"Yes..."

"Well, according to her measurements, she has grown approximately three days in the last twelve hours."

"THREE DAYS?" Diane and I both shouted.

"How is that even possible?" I asked.

"How is any of this possible, Fiona? I just don't know. Your due date is all up in the air now. All I can say is to wait and see what happens. How is your hunger progressing?"

"I think I'm ok, as long as we find Alex tonight. If we don't then I don't know what will happen. We've known for a while now that

Isabella enhances my craving for blood. It's like her hunger controls me..."

Just the thought of blood made my mouth water. My stomach started glowing brighter and my fangs descended into my mouth again. Isabella was hungry and she meant for me to do something about it... soon!

I looked up at Diane and said, "I think it's time that we go. I have the worst feeling that we need to hurry." Diane nodded and Sam started wiping the gel off of my stomach.

Sam was reaching over me to remove a wire that I had missed earlier. I could smell her blood. I could hear her heart beating. I could hear her breathing. I could feel her body heat. Her neck was only inches from my face. My breathing sped up, my pulse increased, and my hunger rose.

My fangs forced themselves into my mouth. I ran my tongue over their tips. My mouth was watering with anticipation of the sweet, red liquid that was flowing through the pulsing vein in Sam's neck.

I opened my mouth wide. I tried not to, but I was not in control of my own body. I tried to say something, but all that came out was a cross between a growl and a hiss. I went in for the kill. Luckily, my noise drew enough of Sam's attention to make her rise up and ask, "What was that? Did you say something?"

Once she saw what I had really been trying to do, she jumped back with a look of pure terror on her face. "What the hell are you doing!" she screamed at me.

Her scream jolted me from my hunger and I realized what had almost happened. "Oh my God! I am so sorry! Are you ok? I didn't hurt you did I? Oh Sam, if I hurt you I'll never forgive myself. Please tell me that you forgive me!" I was sobbing wildly and Sam was so shaken up.

Diane came over and slapped me right across the face. It wasn't a mean slap or anything, just a slap to sort of bring me back to my senses. "Stop it Fiona! Snap out of this bullshit and let's go get that damn husband of your's so that this won't happen again!" See? Passionate = Cussing like a sailor.

"OUCH! Damn it, Diane! Sam, please tell me that you forgive me. I'm not myself today. Please?"

Sam shook her head. She was wringing her hands together and trying to calm herself. I knew that I had scared her and I hated that.

"In all these years of working with vampires, not one time have I had anyone try to bite me. Not in fifteen years. Never!" She shook her head again before running her fingers through her hair. Finally she took a deep breath, stiffened her spine, and stood up as straight as a board. "Yes, ok, I forgive you. We will discount this as a hormonal side effect of this crazy pregnancy. But, let's not have this happen ever again. Do I make myself clear?"

She looked at me with those stern blue eyes and I was instantly hypnotized. I would have done anything that she asked of me just to get her to forgive me. "Yes, of course! Never happen again. Cross my heart. I promise!"

"Ok, if all of this lovey-dovey, mushy crap is over, can we get the hell out of here? You have a husband to rescue if I'm not mistaken, and I have a husband waiting for me at home who thinks I'm simply visiting a sick friend in the hospital." Diane was ready to go. "The sooner we get this over with, the better I'll feel about it all."

I finished getting dressed and Diane brought my shoes over to me. I put them on—with a little help since I can't exactly bend over—and then we were off. Sam wished us luck and demanded that I come back tomorrow so she could check me out again. I shouted an, "ALRIGHT!" as we ran out the door.

Diane brought her minivan around. Yes, we were going vampire hunting in a white minivan. We couldn't have been more of a target if we'd just driven up and shouted, "Come out, come out where ever you are!"

I jumped in and we were on our way. I pulled out the map, traced our route, and then traced a back route so that we could get to the cabin as quickly as possible. Diane was driving eighty and I was holding on for dear life—she's a natural born speed demon when she's not in a hurry so this wasn't much worse than simply going shopping with her on a Saturday morning.

Diane had estimated that it would take us nearly an hour to get to the warehouse district of the neighboring town, but with her driving it only took us thirty-five minutes. When I mentioned it to her she said, "Well, I had to make up the time you wasted trying to take a sip of Sam."

"Bitch." I teased.

"Blood-sucking whore!" she retaliated.

"Hey now! I'm not a whore, I'm a married woman." I stated for the record.

Diane burst out in laughter before declaring that we were in the right place. We drove slowly down alleyway after alleyway until we found the right abandoned warehouse. Diane parked her lovely Mommy-Shuttle and we jumped out as fast as we could.

The sun was almost down, but you could still see a few rays of light over the horizon. We were only minutes from the reanimation of all local vampires. We needed to hurry.

"Grab those flashlights behind the seat!" Diane shouted. I did what she asked and then looked over to where she was standing, only to find that she was loading a pistol.

"Oh hell, where did you get that thing? Does David know that his wife is packing?"

"Yes, he knows, but he doesn't know that I brought it with me to the hospital. When you said Alex was missing, I figured there'd be some shit going down tonight. It's better that we be as protected as we can."

She didn't even look up at me. She just kept right on loading the bullets into their chambers until she clicked everything back into place and shoved the gun into the back of her jeans.

"I hope the safety is on. I'd hate to see you blow your ass off with that thing."

"Oh shut up Fiona; let's get this done."

I turned on one of the flashlights, handed the other to Quick Draw Diane, and we headed into the warehouse.

Chapter 12

I could smell blood, but wasn't sure if it was my body playing tricks on me or if there really was blood in here. The warehouse was dark, dank, and cold. If Alex was in here, he would certainly be freezing—as much as starving—to death.

Diane and I slipped from room to room as quietly as we could. I heard something squeaking in one corner and when I focused the light on that spot I saw that it was only a rat. My adrenaline was pumping and Diane was as jumpy as a child on a trampoline.

When we came upon a door that had a stairway leading down into what was presumably the basement, I knew that Alex had to be down there. Where else would a vampire hold another vampire hostage? A dark, moldy basement is where!

"PSST! Diane, down here" I whispered as loudly as I felt safe doing.

Diane had been looking into another room and my calls out to her made her jump enough that she fired off a round. I jumped at the echoing sound of the gunshot and my hands started glowing with fire. I tried to calm my unborn child, "Shhh, Isabella. Not yet, my sweet. That was just Auntie Diane acting like a scaredy cat. Shhhh." The fire in my hands slowed until it was completely gone.

"Damn it, Diane! Pay attention and stop wave that thing around! If the vampires are awake, you just drew them straight to us. Come on, let's get down there. I know Alex has to be here." I started down the stairs with Diane apologizing in hushed tones behind me the whole time.

When we were almost to the bottom, I saw some lights flickering so I motioned for Diane to shut up and stay back behind me. I felt my heart pounding in my chest. The sound echoed in my ears like tribal drums at an Indian rain dance.

I could feel beads of sweat starting to materialize across my forehead. But, my hands were as steady as a surgeon's hands during a heart transplant. I would find my husband and we would get out of here...

"Do you see anything", Diane asked in a whisper.

I peered around the corner and saw a woman standing at a kitchen sink. The room appeared to be some sort of cafeteria-style break room from when the warehouse was in operation. The woman stretched and yawned like a lazy feline. She was lovely, with the figure of an Egyptian queen.

This woman was slender with an athletic build—certainly weighing less than me, even before I got pregnant—and she moved with the grace of a ballerina. She had long, wavy, blonde hair that

sparkled with health and vigor. She was about an inch taller than me
and her skin was much paler than mine. I knew in an instant that she
was a vampire, which meant that no matter how pretty she was, she
was a dangerous murderer who'd probably rather rip your throat out
than hear you say hello to her.

Diane stumbled on something behind me. I turned around to
give her 'the look' and then turned back around, only to come face-
to-face with the she-demon. She grabbed me by the throat and drug
me out of the safe confines of the shadows and into the room, before
slamming my back up against a wall and holding me there.

"Why look who we have here! If it isn't Alexander's bitch!" She
snarled with her fangs fully distended.

She brought her face close to mine and then sniffed my hair, face,
and neck. "Ah, you smell as sweet as molasses." She paused to
moan her approval. "It's no wonder Alexander claimed you as his
own."

I heard a click in Diane's direction. The woman's eyes darted
toward the sound; my own eyes followed. Diane was standing there
holding her fully-loaded weapon (minus the one round) and pointing
it in my direction. "Let... let go! You let go of my friend!" Diane
demanded in an uneasy, wavering semi-shout.

"Ah, tut tut," the female was wagging her finger in Diane's
direction. "You don't want to do that. You don't want to risk hitting
the little mama." She grabbed my stomach with her free hand and
squeezed so hard that I grimaced in pain. It felt like her nails were
digging into my skin.

94

"I mean it! You let her go or... I will fire!" Diane knew that the bullets wouldn't stop a vampire, but it seemed to give her comfort to say that she would do that.

Just then, I felt my neck released and looked over to find Diane in the choke hold instead. Boy, this bitch could move fast. I heard Diane gasping to breathe and knew that I had to do something, but I didn't want to kill this vampire until she told me where Alex was.

I rushed up behind her—she didn't know that I could move nearly as fast as a vampire—I grabbed her by the hair and drug her off of Diane. Diane fell to the floor, holding her neck and coughing to catch her breath. I drug the vampire across the room; all the while she was kicking, screaming, and trying to pry my fingers out of her hair.

I felt my hands growing warm, but I wasn't ready for that yet. "No, not yet Isabella. Not yet!" I shouted.

I threw the vampire down on the floor and jumped on top of her with my full body weight. She started to grab for my throat again, but I punched her in the face quick enough to deter her actions. She laid there looking up at me with her face twisted into a look of hatred and her fangs showing.

"WHERE IS ALEX?" I demanded to know. She didn't speak, and her silence annoyed me, so I punched her in the face again. Blood started to trickle down the side of her mouth, but she just laughed.

"You aren't a normal human, are you? You're something different. What would that be?" she asked.

"None of you damn business! Where is Alex?" Yet again she didn't answer me so I reared my fist back to give it another go.

"NO! Ok, I'll tell you where he is, if you tell me something first."

I was intrigued, so I said, "Why the hell not? What do you want to know, bitch?"

"What are you? What piqued Alexander's curiosity enough for him to choose someone like you? And how the hell is it possible that you are carrying his child?" She seemed sincere in her curiosity, but for all I knew this was how she intended to catch me off guard and then kill me.

"That was three somethings. But since you're about to die, I'll go ahead and answer them. I was a werewolf. Alex claimed that my unusual scent drew him to me, and when he finally saw me he knew that he had to have me. I was a little less than thrilled about him at first, but he came to my rescue when my pack turned against me.

Alex ended up having to turn me in order to save my life. When he did so, my werewolf DNA combined with his and, somehow, began to reanimate certain parts of his anatomy. That same werewolf DNA somehow blocked some of the vampirisms in my own body and I only received certain traits of a normal vampire."

I waited a moment to see how she would react, but she just laid there waiting on me to finish. "As for our child, Alex's sperm was something that had been regenerated. We had sex and then, ta-da, I was knocked up with the best of 'em."

I looked down at my stomach, for just a split-second, and felt such great love for the person Alex and I had created. It was starting to feel like ages since I last saw his face and felt his arms around me,

96

when in actuality it had only been a day. The bitch took that short moment to make her move. She flipped me off of her and onto the floor. She jumped on top of me and proceeded to punch me in the face as fast and as hard as she could.

"YOU DON'T DESERVE HIM OR HIS CHILD! HE WAS MINE FIRST AND I INTEND ON TAKING HIM BACK!" She was screaming wildly and flailing wildly.

I didn't know who this woman was, but I knew that I had to get her off of me. I heard Diane's gun fire three shots, but that didn't even slow this blonde bimbo's attacks. I heard Diane fire two more shots and then the gun went click, click, click.

The vampire stopped punching me and focused her attention to my stomach. Her hands started circling my unborn baby and I felt her nails scratching my stomach while she was doing it. I screamed, "Who are you and what do you want?"

"I am Serena! I will have him back! I will take this child from your womb and he will be with me forever!"

Just then she took her right hand and dove all four fingers into the flesh of my side. It was like she was trying to scoop out the baby like a spoon scooping up ice cream. I screamed from the pain and started kicking and writhing under her, but she just punched me in the face again with her other hand.

I could feel her fingers moving through my flesh and making their way toward my womb. I could not let her pierce my child's sanctuary. I would not allow it!

I felt the heat rising. My stomach started to glow. Serena jerked her fingers from my body as fast as she could. She jumped up off of me and I slowly climbed to my feet. I could feel the heat flowing through my body; slowly building in strength and intensity.

"Serena, you have made a terrible mistake. You will pay for that mistake, but before you die, could you so kindly tell me where you are keeping my HUSBAND?" I stayed calm enough to keep the power from being discharged.

"Wha... what the hell are you?" Serena stammered in confusion.

"I'm the woman Alex chose, the woman carrying his child, and the woman who is going to kill you and anyone else who stands in my way. I'm the woman who will take her man home tonight, feed from him, and have as much sex as possible with him for the rest of our immortal lives."

Oh, she was steaming now. I was hoping that she would attack so that I could kill her a little faster, but she just stood there. She looked around to see if she could escape, but she would have to go through me in order to reach the stairway or Diane. There was only one door left for her to run for, and I hoped that I could burn her down before she made her way through it.

"Ha! You think he loves you? He loves nothing and no one! He didn't love me when we were together all those decades ago. He cares for no one but himself. I don't care what he tells you, he'll never love you or that abomination in your womb!" She was screaming and pointing her finger at me. I could tell that she was about to dart, so I carefully controlled one small burst of fire from my right hand and threw it down at her feet. She jumped back and screamed.

"You see that? That is what this 'abomination', as you call her, can do. She can remove demons like you from this earth in an instant. Her father and I will make sure that she grows up knowing that fiends like you have no place here!"

She didn't say another word. She looked from side to side and tried to gauge if she could reach the door before I caught her. I knew that she probably could, but I didn't show any doubt on my face. Plus if she ran, I knew that she'd run straight to Alex.

Suddenly, she looked me square in the eyes and a small smile crept across her lips. I knew she was going to do it. She winked at me and then turned and darted for the door. I took off after her, flinging fireballs from both hands over and over—each one missing their target by mere inches. I wasn't really trying to hit her... yet. I wanted her to lead me to Alex.

I glanced over my shoulder to see if Diane was following, but instead saw her huddled in the same spot I'd left her. She'd be alright for now. If there were any other vampires in the vicinity, I would be attracting them to my location so quickly that no one would even notice her anyway.

Chapter 13

Serena was running like the wind. She led me down this long hallway lined on both sides with doors. Alex could be in any one of these and here I was chasing this stupid ass bitch!

As she ran down the hallway, I heard her screaming out for Sebastian. VOILÁ! It was Sebastian after all. I knew this was the right place.

"SEBASTIAN! SEBASTIAN, COME QUICK! HELP ME!" she screamed over and over until she came to another set of stairs leading even further down into the earth.

She stopped, turned to look at me, before taking flight and sailing down the stairs into the darkness below. I couldn't fly, but I could run nearly as fast as a vampire, so I followed her on foot. Her death would be painful when I caught her. There was no sense in making me run this hard in my condition!

I finally made it to the bottom of the stairway and found no light at all down here. It felt like a dungeon in an old castle. It was dark, cool, and the air was heavy with moisture. At this moment, I was grateful that I had retained my werewolf vision during my change.

I was looking down another hallway, only this one wasn't lined with offices. There was only one single door at the other end and Serena was standing in front of it. My heart skipped a beat from the excitement of finding Alex. I just knew that he had to be in that room and Serena would NOT stop me from getting in there.

"SERENA!" I shouted to the whore at the other end of the hall.

She turned slowly and stiffened her body, ready for battle. "What do you want? Why do you waste your time, energy, and possibly your life coming to search for someone as useless as Alexander?"

I started walking slowly toward her. I didn't want to move too quickly for fear that she would go into a fury like a caged beast and escape again. I wanted her dead and I intended to fulfill that wish before I stepped into the room behind that door.

"I've already told you why I'm here. Are you hard of hearing as well as being a stupid bitch? Did you really think that I'd let you get away from me after you attempted to tear my child from my body? It's one thing to try to take a woman's husband, but when you fuck with her kid you're just bringing a hell storm down on your own head!" I was furious and having a really hard time controlling the fire that was rising throughout my body. My temper was about to explode and I was doing all that I could to restrain it.

At that moment, I saw a flash of realization slide across Serena's face. It's like all of a sudden a light bulb went off and she realized that I WAS going to kill her and that she wasn't going to leave this hallway. She didn't say a word. She stood up straight and tall and whispered something that sounded like a prayer.

I heard screaming coming from the door behind her. I had to get in there. I had to protect Alex.

She turned and started to open the door. I took that opportunity to release the energy that had been building up inside my body in one large, strong burst! It only took about one millisecond for the fireball to reach Serena's head. She turned to look at me right before it hit her and I watched her whole body go up in flames.

It's not like in the movies where the vampire starts screaming and running around the room until the fire consumes enough of them to make their charcoal bodies fall onto the floor. No, this energy that my child was funneling through my body was an instant killer. The moment that the flames touched her skin, she was gone. The body is incinerated with nothing left except a few pieces of ash floating around the room and a small pile on the floor where she stood.

I shook myself out of the horror that I had caused and ran for the half-opened door. I didn't creep in or even cautiously glance inside. No, I just burst right in; I was ready for whatever was on the other side.

I saw Alex face down on the floor with the nasty, savage Sebastian on top of him. Sebastian was biting and punching Alex with all his might. Alex was doing what he could, but I could tell that he was so very weak. I screamed at the demon to release my husband, but he kept right on trying to tear Alex apart.

I threw a fireball at the monster, but he dodged it. Even though I didn't hit him, my weapon did distract him from the blows he was laying down on Alex. He flew straight at me and I catapulted several more fireballs in his direction. Unfortunately, he dodged them all.

He moved so swiftly that he was quickly on top of me. He grabbed me by the throat and lifted me up into the air with him. I couldn't breath; the room was spinning from his speed. I was quickly becoming disoriented. I started to panic with the thoughts that I had come all this way and yet Alex, Isabella, and I would still be killed.

"Ah, it's the beautiful Fiona, come to visit us. What a gracious day! Oh, and look here..." he looked down at my stomach and placed his free hand on it. "What do we have here? A little hell's spawn, maybe?"

I twisted and turned, trying to free myself from his grasp. Then, I thought of Isabella and how I'd only had to touch the werewolves that I had killed all those months ago before I'd known about the pregnancy. But, I was slowly losing consciousness and I couldn't concentrate on conjuring up the fire.

"What? Nothing to say? Ah, Fiona, you are too lovely to be silent. I'd love to hear your thoughts on the death penalty and abortions. Or better yet, I'd love to have you over for dinner sometime! You could tell me all about how it's possible that our Alexander has become a father."

He was so smug and arrogant that I probably would have puked if I'd been able to. He was slowly bringing us back down to the floor. Once I was on my feet he pinned me against the filthy wall.

He glanced over at my poor Alex—all bleeding and torn up on the floor—and then he leaned in close and whispered in my ear, "What do you suppose he would think about me taking his bride on the night after his wedding? I'll bet you're a hellion in bed. And I won't even have to worry about getting you pregnant."

He roared with laughter at his own stupid wit. He leaned back in and licked my neck. He nipped at my earlobe and then he whispered, "Let's see what you can do that has put Alexander under your spell." Sebastian slid his free hand down the front of my pants and dove his fingers into a place that no one except Alex had the right to touch.

Sebastian smiled a cruel smile and then forced his mouth over mine. His tongue forced my lips to part so that it could invade. I felt his fangs scrape against my lips. I squirmed as much as I could—trying to escape his grasp—but he took that as me wanting more.

"Oohh, she likes that does she. How about a little more? Surely I'm bigger than the pitiful soul lying over there on the floor." He removed his hand from my pants and backed away just enough to start tugging at his own pants. He still had me by the throat with his other hand, so he was having trouble getting his pants off. I saw him remove the member that was throbbing for attention. That attention would not come from me though.

Sebastian came closer and pressed his body against me again. He pulled at my pants and managed to get them down around my thighs. I was about to be raped and there was nothing I could do about it. I felt the tip of his penis sliding up the side of my leg. I clawed at his hand around my neck. I tried to scratch his eyes out, but he just laughed.

He kissed me again and then began trying to force himself inside of me. But, I'd have none of that. Just when I thought he would succeed, I managed to raise my knee with enough force to catch him squarely in the groin. He went down and took me with him.

I scrambled to my feet, pulling at my clothes, and coughed, sputtered, and gasped for air. He was lying there on the floor writhing in pain. I kicked him... a lot! I kicked him over and over again. I felt my strength increasing with each blow. I heard bones breaking and I felt flesh caving in from the force of my attack. I didn't want to stop.

I was screaming, "YOU FUCKIN' BASTARD! TRY TO RAPE ME, WILL YOU! YOU DON'T KNOW ME! YOU DON'T KNOW WHAT I CAN DO TO YOU!"

I screamed those words over and over again. I hated him. I wanted to keep hurting him. He rolled himself into a ball and couldn't move away from the speed of my bombardment. I would show him!

Suddenly, I heard Alex moan. That sound brought me out of my fury. I looked down at Sebastian, all bloody, broken, and whimpering like a sad puppy, and I couldn't believe that I had been the one who'd done that to him. It was one thing to toss a fireball at someone and watch them go up in smoke, but it was a completely different—savage, monstrous, cruel—thing to tower over another creature and beat them to a bloody pulp.

But, he had attacked me. He had tried to kill Alex. He probably would have killed me. And heaven only knows what he would have done with Isabella.

I left Sebastian there on the floor and rushed to Alex's side. He wasn't coherent. He couldn't speak, he couldn't move, he couldn't even open his eyes. I pulled him up against me and I cradled his upper body like a child. I rocked him and silent tears started streaming down my face.

My poor Alex, he was beaten so badly. His face was distorted from broken bones and torn flesh. His hands were both broken. His ankles were in shackles attached to the wall. Every inch of flesh that I could see was either bleeding, bruised, or completely missing.

I sat there, holding my man, and just looking around the room trying to figure out what I should do next. Sebastian was still lying where I'd left him. There were no sounds in the room except the moaning from these two men and my own rapid breathing. The air was heavy and smelled of blood. I was so hungry, but there was no time for that.

Just then the realization hit me; I had to feed Alex instead of thinking of my own hunger. I had to get him out of here, one way or another, and my only option was to sacrifice my own desires for his need. My pulse quickened and I looked down at Alex again. The muscles in his tattered face were twitching under what little skin that was left there.

My determination was set in stone at that moment. I lifted my left wrist to my own mouth. I bit deeply into the flesh and felt a gush of warm, life-giving blood fill my mouth. I lowered my wrist to his lips and let it drip into his mouth as quickly as it could. After a few drops, Alex started moving his lips and tongue. He soon began to swallow what was being given.

I watched as his face started healing from the lips outward. The resurrection was smooth and fluid—like spilled water creeping across a kitchen table. I pressed my wrist to his mouth. He opened wide and I felt his lips suction to the wound I had created for him. I could feel him drawing the blood from me as quickly as he could.

I watched as his head healed and then the healing process moved down his neck and over his chest. I removed my wrist from his mouth, laid him down gently, and rushed to his feet to see if I could remove the shackles. We would have to get out of here as fast as we could once he was strong enough. I didn't want to be waiting around when Sebastian regained his senses.

I pulled and jerked at the chains, but they weren't budging. I felt my stomach growing warm again and looked down to see it glowing. It was like Isabella was saying, "Here mom. Try this." So I did.

I focused all of my energy into my hands and tried to pinpoint the chains—staying far enough away from Alex's feet so as to not accidentally catch him on fire. The white light of pure energy started flowing from my hands. I grasped the chains in both hands as tightly as I could. I closed my eyes and felt the chains begin to melt. I felt them getting smaller and smaller in my hands, until there was nothing but a puddle of molten iron on the floor.

I went back to Alex and rubbed his face. He opened his eyes and looked up at me. "Alex? Are you ok? We have to get out of here." I glanced in Sebastian's direction...

Oh hell! Where was Sebastian?! My eyes darted around the room. I scanned the whole room from corner to corner. I even looked up at the ceiling to see if he was about to attack. He was gone!

I felt panic and fear rising in the pit of my stomach. There was an immediate sense of urgency to get us out of here. Poor Diane was still upstairs huddled in a corner. Or at least I hoped she was.

I looked back down at Alex. "We have to get out of here! Get up Alex. Get up now!"

I pulled as hard as I could. Alex slowly climbed to his feet. I threw his arm over my shoulder and placed my own around his waist. He was still injured; it would take another feeding before he'd be fully healed.

Alex tried to say something, but it just came out as an indistinguishable whisper. His vocal cords were crushed so I told him to hush, "It's ok. Just be quiet for me. We have to get out of here."

We walked out of the cell. I glanced down at where Serena had gone up in smoke before we slowly climbed the staircase that would lead us up to the level where Diane was. We had to stop every dozen steps for Alex. He was so very weak, but we had to get out of there... NOW!

We finally made it to the top and I yelled for Diane. She didn't come running, so I yelled again. I figured that Sebastian would have already killed us if he'd wanted to. It's not like we were a pair of sprint runners escaping. We were sitting ducks here, so it didn't make much difference if I yelled for Diane.

After I yelled a third time, I saw Diane peak her head out of a door about twenty feet away. She saw that it was me, and that I was dragging Alex along for the ride, and she came running. "Is it over? Are you ok? What happened to him?"

"Shut up Diane and just help me get him out of here. We have to hurry. I'll explain it all when we are far away from here."

Diane grabbed Alex's other arm and threw it over her shoulders. She grabbed around his waist and together we made our way out of the warehouse and into her van. We placed Alex in the back and then we flew out of there like a bat out of hell.

Chapter 14

    I thought Diane had scared me on the way to the warehouse, but now she was doing over one hundred miles per hour on a road that was posted as only fifty. She was weaving in and out of traffic and slinging us from side to side in the curves. I thought Alex was going to roll off of the seat, so I climbed in the back with him to help hold him steady.

    Alex opened his eyes and looked up at me. I smiled down at him and said, "It's ok, my sweet. You are safe now. I won't let anything happen to you, just rest for now." I rubbed his forehead and he closed his eyes again. I laid my ear against his chest and heard the rhythm of his slowly drumming heart. I found comfort in the fact that it was still beating and that I hadn't lost him.

"Hurry Diane, get us back to the cottage as quickly as you can!"

Poor Diane had gotten into more than she could handle. She was scared beyond compare. You could see her whole body shaking with fear and adrenaline. I felt so sorry for getting her caught up in this mess. She would never be the same after this.

"I'm going as fast as I can, Fiona. We'll be there in a few minutes. Just hang on and I'll get us there when I get us there." Her voice was shaky and broken, but she was still sane and, in the end, that's what counts.

About twenty minutes later, we pulled up outside the cottage. All of the lights were off, but it looked just like we'd left it. I told Diane to stay in the van and lock the doors. I was going to go inside and make sure that Sebastian wasn't in there waiting for us. I kissed Alex and jumped out of the van. She nodded and did just as I asked.

The forest was quiet. There wasn't even a sound of a scurrying possum making its way through the darkness. I peered around in the darkness, listening intently before taking a step further. I scanned the forest with my werewolf vision, but didn't see anything.

I walked toward the house—making sure to go slowly and cautiously. I made it to the front door and quietly turned the knob. I pushed the door and it opened slowly. No one jumped out at me, so I walked inside. I looked around the living room, the kitchen, the spare bedroom and the bathroom... no one was here.

I walked downstairs to our bedroom to look around. The room was just as it had been left—Alex's broken lamp and clothes on the floor from the night before. I lit a candle in the bedroom before walking into the last room in the house to check, my bathroom.

I walked into the bathroom that Alex had built for me. I switched on the light and looked around. The shower was empty, the toilet was still here... what the hell is that? I turned to look into the mirror over the sink. Oh no!

On the mirror—written in my favorite lipstick shade—was a message.

You will pay! I will have your child!
See you soon,
S.

I looked around me, fully expecting Sebastian to jump out at me like in the movies. My heart was racing and I felt panicky. All of a sudden I couldn't breathe. I had to get out of there.

I stumbled out of the bathroom, through the bedroom, and up the stairs. I thought I would pass out before I made it outside. But once I felt the cool, evening air hit my skin, I felt like running.

I dashed over to the van, but couldn't hide how scared I was at that moment. Diane saw the look of horror on my face and asked, "What? What is it? Is there someone in there?!" She started looking around trying to see if someone was outside her van.

I shook my head no and said, "No, not anymore. Just help me get Alex inside, quickly!"

Diane got out of the van and came around to the passenger's side to help me get Alex out of the back. We were pulling him to his feet when I felt a sharp, cringing pain in my stomach. I nearly dropped Alex because of it.

Diane looked at me with concern written all over her face. "Are you ok? Was that a contraction?"

"Don't worry about it. I'm ok," said between deep breaths, "Let's just get him inside." I looked around making sure that no one was around and we proceeded into the house.

"Let's take him downstairs. I don't want to be here alone with it's time for the sun to rise and me trying to get him downstairs alone." Diane nodded and we worked our way down to the bedroom.

We laid Alex on the bed and I motioned for Diane to follow me into the bathroom. Once in there I showed her the mirror. "What do you think of this?" I asked while pointing at the message.

"Oh hell, Fiona. Who's it from? Does the S. stand for Sebastian?" I had forgotten that Diane didn't know what happened in the chamber that I'd rescued Alex from. In hushed tones so that Alex wouldn't hear, I went ahead and told her everything.

I told her about chasing Serena down the stairs and catching her at the bottom. "GOOD! I'm glad that bitch is dead!"

I told her about the almost rape and how I'd gone off on Sebastian. "Well, he deserved it after that! You did the right thing."

She hugged me tightly and then I told her about melting the chains and looking up to find Sebastian gone. "Fuck, Fiona! Now he's out there somewhere, just waiting to catch you off kilter. Who knows what he'll try to do next!"

"Shhhh! I know. That's why I don't want Alex to hear right now. He needs at least the rest of tonight to heal. Then tomorrow I'll tell him and we'll figure it all out."

Just then I had another sharp pain in my stomach. I crumpled over and clasped my hands over my abdomen. My whole stomach felt rock hard and the pain radiated around my stomach and to my back. I could hear Diane asking me if I was alright, but all I could do was breath deeply and wait for it to pass.

"You need to rest Fiona. Those look like contractions to me. And remember that I've done those before, so I should know."

The pain passed and I walked Diane back out to her vehicle. "Are you sure you don't want me to stay? I can call David and let him know I won't be home tonight?"

"No, you've helped me enough tonight. Now go home to your family and squeeze them tightly." I hugged Diane, made her promise to call me the next day, and watched her drive away.

I watched the forest before going back inside. The tree tops were swaying with a light breeze. The animals were either fast asleep or elsewhere savaging for food. The only sound was the rustling of the newly budding sprouts on the trees blowing in the wind. There was nothing but the sweet smell of spring in the air.

I walked back inside the cottage and locked the door behind me. I double checked that the back door was locked securely and that all windows were closed. They were, and that made me feel better— even if deep down I knew it wouldn't help. Then I went over to the bedroom door and made sure it was locked. I didn't want anyone getting in and hurting Alex anymore than he already was.

I decided to build a fire in the fireplace. It took a few minutes of coaxing, but I finally got the flames to stir and flicker enough to burn the wood. I wasn't really cold, but there's something soothing about

114

watching flames dance and twirl on their own paths and in their own rhythm.

I walked into the kitchen to make myself a mug of hot chocolate. Thank goodness for microwaves and packets of instant hot chocolate. I love those little marshmellows and the clumps of undissolved chocolate that you always find in the bottom of the mug. So in a matter of two minutes I had a nice, steaming mug of sweetness in my hands.

I slowly made my way back to the living room, and had just sat down on the couch, when I had another pain in my stomach. I almost dropped my mug of yummy goodness because of it. I knew that these were contractions, but I refused to announce them to the world for fear that making them known would make them real to me. I refused to give birth to this little girl while her daddy was downstairs healing from a near-death beating dealt him by a monster who wanted to take them both from me.

The longer I held out on allowing the presence of these contractions to be known, the longer I had to figure out how to deal with this horrid situation. Don't get me wrong, I knew that I didn't have an indefinite amount of time here. But, I also knew that I most likely had quite a while before things became so dire that I would need the assistance of another, or at least I hoped so.

The pain passed, so I decided to curl up with my favorite blanket to drink my hot chocolate and just watch the fire. I pulled the blanket up close and deeply inhaled the scent of Alex that was left behind from our last cuddle session. I laid back on the couch and took a sip of the hot chocolate. The fire was sparkling, flickering, and crackling. Each incandescent flame was licking at its own special spot on the logs. The smell of burning wood was soothing and I hoped the logs would burn slowly.

I was so tired that I just laid there. Once my hot chocolate was gone, I sat the mug in the floor and slid the rest of the way down on the couch. I laid there on my left side, hugging tightly to the blanket, and my eyelids felt so heavy. I just needed to sleep. I'd been awake for so long and I had used too much of my energy to rescue Alex.

I rubbed my right hand over my abdomen and felt the life within squirming around. She would be released from her cramped prison far too soon for my liking. I was thrilled at the prospect of meeting her, but I just wasn't ready yet.

The child within kicked her tiny foot in the direction of my slumbering hand. I felt the flesh beneath stretching and pulling from the force of that little creature. I wished that Alex was awake so that he could feel this. He loves watching our child cause turbulent waves and ripples from within my body.

There were still marks on my stomach from Serena thrusting her fingers into me. Luckily, I was a fast healer so they should be gone by the morning. Even if they were gone, I would never forget them. They were forever burned into my memory as the moment I nearly lost our baby to that demon bitch.

I felt my eyes closing, I knew that I was falling asleep, and there was nothing I could do about it. I needed to go be with Alex, but my body had other plans. I felt like I was floating and fierce scenes began to tumble through my head. I saw Serena digging her claws into my body, Alex lying lifeless on the dungeon floor, and Sebastian trying to take a part of me that I was not offering. I knew that I wouldn't sleep well until this was all over.

Chapter 15

When I awoke it was already morning. I had slept on the couch all night. The fire was out and there was a little chill in the cottage. My heart was heavy from the nightmares that had plagued me all night.

I could hear birds chirping—oblivious to everything that had happened the night before. My stomach growled and I knew that I'd have to at least try to eat some real food this morning. Maybe Alex would feel up to sharing when he wakes later.

I yawned and began to stretch—like I do every morning—but my stretch was forcibly halted by pains throughout my whole body. Every inch of me ached with soreness. My hands felt like they had arthritis in them. My ribs felt like someone had used them as a punching bag. My feet felt like I'd been in high-heeled shoes for several days in a row. Even my hair seemed to hurt. It was like my nightmare encounters had ravaged my body worse than real life had.

I started to sit up, but every muscle that was used in the process started screaming at me with disapproval. I laid back and tried to catch my breath from the pain. I knew that I needed to get up, but, on top of the pain, even my eyes were in protest of the rays of sunlight streaming in through the windows.

I decided to stay there on the couch for a few more minutes. I was working up my courage to force my body into animation when I heard a *tap, tap, tap* at the front door. It was only a few feet from where I was laying, but I didn't see myself making it over there easily.

"Who is it?" I shouted to the visitor.

"It's Sam. Let me in."

"Come on in, Sam. I'm having issues this morning." I was stiffer than a broomstick.

Sam jiggled the door knob, but it was locked. Alex & I had given her a key as soon as we found out I was pregnant. We didn't know how things would go with the pregnancy and you never know when your doctor might need to come in without you being the one to open the door. So after a moment of listening to Sam complain about having too many keys on her key ring and how she can never find what she's looking for, she finally made it through the door.

"What the hell is wrong? Why didn't you open the door for me? I can never find anything on this damn key ring," Sam said as she closed the door behind her and walked toward my direction.

"What happened last night? Diane called me early this morning to tell me that I should come over to check you out. Are you ok? Why are you lying on the couch at this time of day?"

"Well, it was a long night and I fell asleep here. Then when I woke up a few minutes ago... well, nothing works."

Sam looked puzzled, "What do you mean 'nothing works'?"

"I mean, I can't move. Everything hurts. Nothing is working correctly and I'm soooo sore."

"Well, let's check you out then." Sam sat down on the side of the couch and pulled out the stethoscope from her ever-present black bag and proceeded to check my stats.

"Everything appears to be alright with your pulse and blood pressure. Where are you sore at?"

I made a large sweeping motion with both of my hands to symbolize that my whole body hurts. "Everywhere! It all aches more than I've ever hurt before."

"Well, let's see if we can get you into a warm tub of water and just let your muscles soak for a while." Sam began trying to help me off of the couch and I started moaning and groaning in utter pain.

We finally made it into the bathroom—after having to take tiny, baby steps all the way there. Then Sam sat me on the toilet while she filled the tub of water that was at just the right temperature for my pregnant body. Of course, I found that quite ironic considering my fetus could give off her own heat in much larger doses than a simple household water heater could.

As I sat there, I vaguely recall hearing Sam rambling on about taking care of myself, how I looked much larger this morning than I had yesterday and something about eating some real food for a change. All the while I was sitting there remembering the first night that Alex had bathed me in that very tub. My mind had been against it, but my body was all for it. As I looked down at my gigantic stomach, I knew that I would be forever grateful that my body had won out in that debate.

"Fiona? Fiona, are you listening to me?"

I was startled for a moment, but looked up at Sam to see her standing over me like an evil stepmother.

"Hello? Wake up Ms. Daydreamer. Your bath is ready. Do you think you can manage to get in? Or should I help you?" She was completely serious... in a doctor kind of way.

"Would you? I really doubt I'll be able to easily accomplish getting in there. Hell, I can barely do it in this condition when I'm NOT hurting all over."

So Sam helped me undress and climb into the tub. The water was so warm and inviting. The heat started soothing my body almost instantly.

Sam said that she was going to go fix me some breakfast and for me to give a yell when I was ready to get out. I watched her leave, closing the door behind her, and heard her begin to bang around in the kitchen. I just laid back in the water and thought about everything that had happened, and would happen.

My life had been in a whirlwind of extreme unexpectedness since the day I first laid the sense of smell on Alex. But, I didn't regret any of it. Sure, I didn't plan to die, be brought back to life, and fall in love with a vampire. I also didn't plan to become pregnant with a little person who shouldn't exist. And as much as I wanted to believe that I knew what the future would hold, I didn't.

I laid there just soaking like a chicken in a stewpot, and then I felt an odd sensation of peace wash over me. At that moment, I knew that everything would be alright. I didn't know how and I didn't know when, but I knew that in the end I would be happy... if only for a moment.

Suddenly, I heard a frantic scream coming from the kitchen. I darted up out of the water faster than I thought I could possibly move in the state I was in. I threw on a robe and dashed out the door. The pain was being doused by adrenaline and the fear that someone was hurting Sam.

When I rushed into the kitchen, I saw Sam standing in front of the open fridge, staring down at something lying on the floor at her feet.

"What?!" I yelled to her. She didn't speak. She just kept looking down and started pointing at whatever was on the floor.

I walked around her so that I could see what the hell had gotten her so spooked, and there lay Alex's pet rabbit. The one creature that he always took prestigious care of... aside from me, of course! He swore that he only kept it around in case of an emergency, but I'd only ever heard of him needing to feed from it once since we've been together. He always fed it like a king, bathed it, and even brushed its fur on occasion.

The poor bunny was lying there covered in what appeared to be its own blood. It looked mangled—like it had been run through a lawn mower—and it was so obviously dead. I kneeled down to get a closer look, or to get some sense of what I was going to tell Alex, when I noticed something white sticking out from under it.

I carefully slipped my fingers under the mangled mess and pulled out what turned out to be a piece of paper. It had blood all over it, but you could still make out the writing. Sam was watching me and when she spotted the paper she asked what it said. So I read it aloud.

"Here lies Braxton Bunny. He was a good guy who left us far too soon. If only his owners had realized that he would become vampire food. With love, Sebastian"

I dropped the paper like it was a snake preparing to strike. I was appalled by what I had just read. Sebastian had not only left his mark on the bathroom mirror downstairs, but he had killed Alex's rabbit and then had time to shove it into our refrigerator and leave a note.

When did this happen? Before we got back, like the mirror? Or after we were home and I was sleeping on the couch. The thought of him coming into the house while I was sleeping was enough to make me rush to the bathroom and vomit.

When I came back out of the bathroom I saw Sam squatting down to clean up the mess. I wasn't about to stop her, but I felt awful that she had simply come over to help out and was left with that. I doubted that this would be the worst of it though.

"Thank you so much, Samantha. You just don't even realize how much I appreciate you."

"Oh get on with it, Fiona. It's no bother. I was just surprised by the appearance of a deceased woodland creature in your fridge. Of course, I guess I shouldn't have been surprised with everything that

has been going on lately, and you and Alexander being what you are."
She chuckled from her own wit and went back to her work.

"You do realize that we don't eat 'woodland creatures', right?
Sam just rolled her eyes and continued cleaning up the deceased
bunny.

I decided that I would go downstairs to check on Alex. I told
Sam and she shooed me away with the promise of a full breakfast as
soon as she was finished cleaning up. I hated the thought of having
to tell Alex about his rabbit. But knowing him, he would be stoic
and act like he didn't care a whip about his beloved pet.

I was walking out of the kitchen when I had another sharp pain. I
gasped loudly from the suddenness of it and hurried around the
corner so that Sam wouldn't see me.

"Is everything alright out there?" Sam shouted from the kitchen.

"Yes, I just stubbed my toe," I said through gritted teeth.

After a minute or two of leaning against the wall and doing some
deep breathing, I straightened back up and headed downstairs. I had
to be careful not to open the door too widely for fear that a stray
beam of sunlight might slip into the room. I certainly wouldn't want
Alex waking up with burns after all the trouble we went through to
rescue him.

I slipped down the stairs and into the bedroom. Alex was
sleeping peacefully and it appeared that all of his visible wounds had
healed completely. I slipped under the covers and slid over next to
him. His cool body was as still as a boulder, and nearly as solid as
one.

I slid my hand under the single satin sheet that covered his body from the waist down and rubbed his thigh. Any other time this simple act would conjure up a need so fierce within him that he'd be on top of me in a matter of seconds—with me cackling in delight the entire time. But, with him dead to the world around him, nothing happened.

I slid my hand over his stomach—lingering over those rock hard abs that I loved so much—before settling above his slowly beating heart. I just laid there, cuddled up tightly to him, and waited. I didn't know what I was waiting for, but I knew that I should just wait.

I looked up at his face and saw the shadow of masculinity, which he was so proud of, on his face. It always made me snicker when he would talk about how much he loved being able to grow facial hair these days, and yet he can't wait to rush right off and shave it. Men!

"Please be alright, Alex," I whispered in his ear, "I can't do this without you. Your child will not delay her birth much longer and I need you by my side when it happens."

I heard Sam yelling for me to come and eat, but I wasn't ready to leave Alex's side. I snuggled up closer and nuzzled his neck. Suddenly, the urge to feed was too much to handle. It had been more than a day and a half since I'd fed last AND I'd let him take from me during that time. I was soooo hungry for his blood that I couldn't control it any longer.

I felt my fangs extending into my mouth. It felt like an eternity since I'd used them last. They filled my mouth and I slid my tongue across the tips. They were ready for action and I wasn't about to refuse. Alex wouldn't mind; he was sleeping after all.

I crawled up on top of him, straddled his waist, and turned his head to the left so that I'd have free reign of his neck. I leaned in close and inhaled his scent, deeply. I licked his neck slowly; wishing he were awake to join in on the fun.

I slowly punctured his cold flesh with my fangs and felt the blood begin to slowly trickle into my mouth. The pure ecstasy that I felt in that moment was almost orgasmic. The blood slid down the back of my throat with the ease of chocolate pudding. It was sweet and salty, with a touch of bitterness all at the same time.

I fed until the hunger started to subside. I felt so much better, and I realized that I hadn't noticed a single contraction the whole time I'd been down here with Alex. I wondered if that would work when I went into hard labor.

I climbed off of Alex and headed toward the bathroom to clean up. I turned on the lights, and was punched in the gut with the reminder of what had transpired the night before. There, on the mirror, was Sebastian's message. I couldn't believe that I had forgotten to clean that off last night.

I pulled out my cleaning supplies from under the sink and proceeded to scrub the lipstick from the glass. My scrubbing became frantic when the words just wouldn't come off.

"Why the hell won't you come off?" I shouted.

My heart was racing, but I managed to smear every word until they were unreadable. I didn't want to see those words anymore. I just wanted them gone. I didn't want to even think about Sebastian at the moment. I knew that my child would be born soon, and the thought of even his words being nearby scared me more than I cared to admit to anyone.

Satisfied with the mess on the mirror, I dropped the sponge into the sink and just walked out. No one would be able to read what had been there and I wasn't in the mood to think about it any longer. I walked through the bedroom—grabbing a nearby towel in the process—and proceeded to clean off Alex's neck and my mouth. I kissed him on the lips and went up the stairs, locking the door behind me.

Once upstairs, I had a nice breakfast with Samantha and endured her constant rambling about me taking care of myself. She insisted that I come with her to the office for yet another ultrasound. "Alex will be sleeping all day anyway," she stated. "What else do you have planned to do today?" So I finally agreed and we were off for another checkup, yet again.

Chapter 16

When I awoke, I heard voices coming from above. It must have been early evening—or else I wouldn't be awake. I couldn't imagine what was going on up there at this time of day though.

I felt the softness of the bed beneath me before I even opened my eyes. I could tell that I was home, and not in hell. I sat up in bed and looked around the room. The last thing that I clearly recalled was being in Sebastian's dungeon of torture. I remembered him kicking, biting, punching, and clawing at every inch of me. Then there was a flash of heat and light and all went quiet.

Oh wait! I did remember glimpses of Fiona's sweet face. I remembered her saying to be quiet and I think I remembered seeing a flash of Diane. But after that there was nothing. How had I gotten home? Better yet, how had Fiona accomplished getting me downstairs?

I rose from the bed and went to the bathroom to splash some water on my face. Instead, I was welcomed by red lipstick smeared all over the mirror. So in a flash, I picked up an abandoned sponge from the sink and removed every last speck of red from the mirror.

I started to go upstairs, but quickly recalled the voices I had heard. So I threw on some pajama pants and slowly headed in the direction of the voices. Before I reached the top, I noticed a little aching feeling on my neck.

I ran my hand over it and realized that it was two small puncture wounds. I went back to the mirror to take a look. It appeared that Fiona had required sustenance before I was awake to give it. Hmmm, she's never done that before.

I finally made it upstairs and cautiously peered around the corner and into the living room—where all of the noise was coming from. There, on the couch, was Fiona, Diane, and Samantha. To the left, in a chair, there was a woman that I recognized as one of Samantha's assistants.

I watched as the three women fawned all around Fiona. The conversation seemed to be geared toward our unborn child and her untimely arrival. I was listening intently when I heard Samantha say, "Fiona, you can't hold her in. She will come one way or another. Please, can't we just take you to the hospital and leave Alex a note?"

I stepped around the corner and asked, "What's this I hear about going to the hospital?"

Fiona's face brightened up. She ran over to me, before jumping onto me and wrapping her arms around my neck. "Oh, Alex! You're awake! I was so afraid that I'd never hear your voice again!" Tears were streaming down her face and I just hugged her tightly until she was ready to release me.

I lowered her to her feet and held her close. "I'm here, my love. It's ok. Don't cry. You know I hate it when you do that." I wiped the tears from her cheeks and kissed her tender lips ever so lightly. She laid her head on my chest and just clung to me like her life depended on it.

After a moment, I heard Samantha start to speak, "Alex, we are in a dire situation here. Fiona has been in early labor for about a day now, but she refuses to let me take her to the hospital. She's been waiting for you to wake up so that she'll know that you're alright."

Samantha waited a moment, and when Fiona didn't respond, she said, "You two need to talk... now. Diane, Francis..." Samantha thumbed toward the doorway and then all three walked out of the living room in a single file line and headed for the kitchen.

I looked down at Fiona. Her complexion was so pale; very unlike her. I could see worry all over her face. I led her over to the couch and we sat.

"What has happened? How did I get away from Sebastian? What's going on with the baby?" I was firing off questions, but Fiona just sat there with her hands in her lap and her head slightly bowed.

"Fiona, my sweet, my love, mother of my child, please tell me what is going on here. I must know."

I grabbed her hands and held them tightly in my own. She was so warm that I held them up my cheek and closed my eyes while she caressed my face. When I reopened my eyes, there was Fiona staring back at me. She had that look of love on her face again, but it was mingled with fear and maybe a touch of pain. I rubbed her cheek and waited for her to talk to me.

"Alex, I came for you last night. I brought Diane with me and we came for you. I killed the one called Serena..."

"You killed Serena?" I asked, full of surprise. She nodded and I asked, "How was that even possible?"

Fiona looked down at her stomach and then back up at me. I understood completely. Our child had taken care of Serena. I had always sensed that Fiona's power was pregnancy-related and not hers completely.

"Ok, what else happened? How did you get me away from Sebastian? Why did he not kill you?"

I could tell that she didn't want to tell me what was going on, but she continued anyway. "Well, after I killed Serena, I came upon Sebastian killing you. He was literally killing you. He looked like a wild animal with rabies or something. He was flying all around you, tearing you apart."

She stopped, but I didn't want her to. "And?"

"Well, then he spotted me. He attacked me. Then... "

"Go on, my love. Then?"

"Before I tell, I want you to stay calm. Ok?"

I nodded and said, "Alright, just tell me."

"He tried to rape me. He was almost successful, but I stopped him and ended up beating the shit out of him in the process. As he was lying there on the floor moaning in pain, I came to your side and fed you enough so that you'd be able to walk." Fiona had said all of that so quickly that it took me a moment to understand exactly what she had said.

When it finally hit me, I couldn't believe what I had heard. Sebastian had tried to rape my Fiona! I would kill him with my bare hands. He wouldn't have a chance to do such a thing again.

Fiona just sat there, letting what she had said sink into my brain. I knew that there had to be more, but I needed a minute to process and check my anger. I balled my fists up, rose from the couch, and started pacing the room. All I could think about was him touching her, him doing things to her against her will, him touching my wife in ways the only I should be allowed to touch her.

Fiona didn't wait for me to calm down. I suppose she figured it better to just get it over with. "Alex, when I was working on melting the chains that were binding your ankles to the wall, Sebastian escaped. He was there lying on the floor one minute, and then he was gone the next. As soon as I got you free I high-tailed it out of there with you and Diane at my side."

I paced the floor, full of anger. I wanted to yell, hit, and break something. I looked at Fiona; she was sitting there with her hands folded in her lap. I'd never seen her so frightened in all the time we'd been together. She had her head bowed and I thought I saw the glistening of a tear forming in the corner of one of those lovely

132

brown eyes. That's all it took for me to calm to the point of being able to speak softly to her.

"But, I don't understand how you found me, or what happened during the daylight hours after I was gone. How did you make it to where I was, without getting caught or killed? There are a lot of details missing here, my love," I cooed lovingly. "Oh, and what's this about you being in early labor?"

"Alex, don't worry about all of that. I will explain all of the nitty-gritty details later. For now, you need to know that Sebastian is still out there and he's coming for us."

I stopped pacing and looked right at Fiona. "What do you mean that he's coming for us? I know he's an angry creature, but what makes you think he's coming after us?"

"Did you happen to see the smeared lipstick on the bathroom mirror?"

"Yeah, I cleaned it off, but..."

"Well, it was a message from Sebastian. He left it there before we even made it back from the warehouse that he was holding you in. He had been inside the house, yet again. First he came in and took you and then he left that message. Then... "

Her voice trailed off. She rose from the couch and walked over to me. She held both of my hands and looked up into my eyes. "He came in a third time. I don't know if it was at the same time as the mirror or if it was later after we were home and I was sleeping on the couch. Either way, he left another message."

"What? What did he leave that time? What did the mirror message say also?"

"The mirror message said that he was coming to get the baby."

"THE HELL HE IS!" I interrupted.

"The second message was your rabbit."

I was confused. "Huh? What does my rabbit have to do with anything? What about the rabbit?" I asked.

"Well, he killed your rabbit and put it in the refrigerator. He left a little poem saying that the rabbit had been vampire food." She hugged me tightly and then conveyed her condolences. "I'm so sorry sweetie. I know how much you cared about the rabbit."

"Forget about the rabbit. Our child has been threatened. You have been attacked and I would have been killed if you hadn't shown up. This can not go on. I must make a statement now to all vampires, big and small, that I will not tolerate such acts against my own!"

I kissed Fiona on the forehead cupped her face in my hands and continued, "You don't have to worry about anything like this happening again. I will take care of it."

Suddenly, Fiona doubled over with pain. She was clasping her stomach and her breathing increased to a pant. Fiona really was in labor!

I picked her up and carefully laid her on the couch. I rubbed her hair out of her face and lightly kissed her cheeks. There was no way I could leave her like this. She needed me, now more than ever. Sebastian would have to wait, but there was no mistaking that I would have to kill him in order for my wife and child to be safe.

Fiona screamed from the pain and Samantha, Diane, and Francis came running from the other room. They all circled around us and

134

Samantha started checking Fiona's pulse and listening to the baby's heartbeat. Samantha felt around on Fiona's stomach and then she said that she needed to check Fiona's dilation.

Fiona asked Diane and Francis to go make her some tea and they left the room. Samantha then proceeded to check everything that she needed to check. Fiona was so uncomfortable that I hated to just stand by and watch.

"Don't worry Alexander, everything looks good. There will probably be a few hours before your little lady arrives." Samantha was reassuring me the only way that she knew how.

"But, what about Fiona?" I looked down at her and she was beginning to sweat. The heat was radiating from her body. Her face was scrunched up from the pain. She looked like she was scared out of her wits.

Samantha stepped away from Fiona and pulled me along with her. In a low whisper she said, "Fiona is ok. She's too tense right now. She's worried about letting the baby be born with Sebastian out there waiting to take her. She's trying her damnedest to keep your child inside of her. I didn't even know she was in labor until I took her to the office for an ultrasound and I saw the contractions measuring on the machines."

I looked back at my beloved, writhing in pain, and felt horrible about it all. I would have to take care of Sebastian before the baby was born. But, I hated the thought of not being at her side during all of this.

"Alexander, you are going to have to do something to calm her down. See if she'll feed. Or talk to her about something that will relax her. Just do something to calm her down enough for the labor to progress smoothly. The more stressed she is, the more painful the birth will be. And she has refused to go to the hospital so that I can give her the pain medications because she fears that Sebastian will walk in and take the baby from her. She says that her daughter won't leave her arms without him killing her first."

"Alright Samantha, I know what has to be done, now. Fiona won't have to worry about Sebastian any longer." I was calm and knew what I would do. I would take care of this situation so that Fiona could relax and our daughter could be born into the safety of our arms. Things would be resolved, one way or another, by the end of the night.

I dashed downstairs to change clothes and then back upstairs to Fiona's side. Fiona was resting her eyes. She was still having contractions, but in between, she was resting. I kneeled down beside her and whispered in her ear, "I'll be back soon, my love. Can you hold on until I return?"

She opened her eyes slowly and looked up at me with those beautiful brown eyes. A small smile spread across her luscious mouth. Her eyes twinkled with the knowledge of what I was about to do, and she approved.

"Be careful and come back soon. I'll be alright. Sam, Diane, and Francis will be here to help—with all of their child birthing experience. Don't you worry about me, just focus on the task at hand and I'll be here when you return."

Oh, I love this woman. She understands me more than anyone I've ever known. I kissed her forehead. I looked back at Samantha

136

and nodded, told the ladies to take care of my love and out the door I went.

Chapter 17

The contractions were like waves, with peaks and valleys. The valleys were great, easy, and peaceful. But, the peaks were hard, painful, and frantic. I was having trouble focusing on anything except the pain and the fact that Alex wasn't here, but my friends were here to support me and help me through this.

The ladies were running around back and forth from here to the kitchen and to the bathroom. They were making me nervous with all of the activity. I was simply lying on the couch trying to rest between the contractions. They were still pretty far apart and Sam said it would probably be several hours before Isabella would make her appearance—which suited me just fine!

During one of the valleys, I got up, walked around for a few minutes, and made myself a mug of hot chocolate—even though there were several protests from the women-folk. I sat at the kitchen table and soon the three ladies, one by one, seated themselves around me. I thought it a good idea to have a chat with them about what was to come.

"Ladies, we need to talk for a moment." They all looked at me inquisitively, awaiting my continuation. "You all know what Alex is, what I am, and what transpired last night." They all nodded in affirmation. "Well, Alex has gone to take care of our problem named Sebastian." They all nodded again. It seemed that they already knew all of this.

"Fiona, we are here for you. No one knows what Alex is out there doing, but we do know what you're doing. You're busy birthing that sweet baby of yours and you need us here. Alex can take care of himself, but in this situation, you can't. If you are even thinking of going to help him, in your condition, then I must say that I am adamantly against it with all my being." Diane wasn't about to let me run off again after last night.

"I have to concur with Diane. You must stay here and prepare for birth. Or we could go ahead and take you to the hospital and do it all there. It's so much safer there than out here in the middle of nowhere. There are security personnel and all of the equipment we could possibly need." Sam was determined to get me to her hospital.

But, I really wanted to stay here where it was safe for Alex if the sun came up before the baby was born.

"Sam, you know that I want to stay here. Yes, the hospital has security guards and equipment, but this cottage has our sun-tight bedroom for Alex to escape to in case the sun comes up before the birth is over. If it looks like something isn't going quite right, then I will agree to head to the hospital and your machinery. But until then, I will be staying right here. Does everyone understand?"

All three ladies nodded in unison and took turns patting my hand.

"All right, Fiona. We will do whatever you want," agreed Diane.

Sam chimed in with, "Yes, all right, as long as you and the baby look like you're tolerating labor."

Francis just sat there. She didn't talk much, but she was very skilled at doing what she's told and was a complete professional. Not to mention that you couldn't pry a secret out of that woman if you tortured and threatened to burn her at the stake. Don't ask me how I know. Let's just say that I've heard a few stories over the last few months that would make even the strongest stomach queasy.

"Great! Now, let's discuss how this is all going to go down over the next few hours. Alex has gone to kill Sebastian. There! I've said it point blank. If he returns..."

I paused to rephrase my statement. "No, not if... WHEN he returns, he will most likely be in pretty bad shape. After last night, I will be completely shocked if he's not in rough condition."

"What are you proposing, Fiona?" Sam asked.

"Well, Alex will most likely need to feed when he returns home. It's the only way that he will be able to heal from such a beating. So

140

what I'm proposing is that we figure out a way to let Alex feed from me, and I from him, during the labor."

Diane and Sam looked completely and utterly astounded that I would suggest such a thing. Francis just sat there without the slightest change in facial expression. I knew I'd have to explain it to them in a little more detail.

"It's all right, ladies. I found out this morning that feeding from Alex actually helps ease my contractions." I looked Sam, "Remember this morning when I went down to check on Alex? While down there, I fed from him. I was having contractions at that time and as soon as I started feeding the contractions subsided. Or maybe I should say that the pain did."

"Why didn't you mention this earlier? We could have utilized that as a very good pain reliever." Sam was always so clinical.

"Well, because I knew that Alex would want to go off and take care of Sebastian, and I didn't want to stop him. That probably sounds selfish, but I don't care. I want my child born into the safety of our life together, NOT the threats of a crazed vampire!"

"Ok, we'll see what we can do when he returns. But, you have to know that you will be losing blood during the delivery, and then to let him feed will just deplete your supply even more. You will have to feed from him at the same time in order to sustain an acceptable amount of blood and nourishment in your system at all times."

Sam looked deep in thought for a moment before continuing with, "If worst comes to worst I can always allow you to take some from me. I know that you will be in much better control of your faculties than you were yesterday. Starvation can do terrible things to even the best of people."

Wow! Sam was offering me her own blood. And after I had nearly taken it from her, by force, yesterday!

"That is very generous of you Sam, but I've been her best friend since childhood. So she should take what she needs from me."

I grinned at the thought of Diane arguing with Sam on the subject of giving their blood to me. "I appreciate the offers, ladies, but it only works from Alex. Well, as far as I know. I've never fed from anyone except Alex."

Diane couldn't take a polite no for an answer, "Well, if it comes down to it, I want you to take from me. I've got plenty and I'll do anything to ensure your and little Isabella's safety."

I nodded and smiled at my wonderful friend. She was so great. I took the last gulp of hot chocolate and then told them that we had one more thing to discuss.

"Now, I want to talk about a possible contingency plan, in case we are attacked before Alex returns."

"Attacked! What do you mean attacked?" Sam shouted.

"I mean just that, if we are attacked here at the house by another vampire before Alex gets home. We need to have a plan in case Sebastian comes for me, or sends someone else after me. What if Alex is killed and Sebastian isn't? That kind of stuff."

"What should be planned?" Diane asked.

"Ok, I've been thinking about this for a little while and I think I've come up with a good escape plan. First, I want you all to go out and park your cars at the end of the house; closest to the cellar door.

142

Then, we'll move our work station downstairs to the bedroom. I don't want to give birth on the couch, after all." They all nodded in agreement.

"Lastly, we'll lock ourselves down there and hope for the best. If something does happen, we'll escape out to the cars through the cellar door—it's not really blocked off like Alex wants everyone to think. We have a secret door down there behind an unattached wall panel and it leads right out the cellar doors."

"Well, that's as good an idea as any, I suppose. Let's go ladies. Let's get those vehicles moved." Diane was great at dictating when the need arises.

All three went out and moved their cars to just the right spots, and even turned them around so that they were all pointed in the right direction to escape quickly. Diane fixed her van so that the sliding door was closest to the cellar door. That way, they'd be able to throw me in there with as little effort as possible, and off we'd go.

After they all came back in, they went to work moving all of the birthing supplies, a microwave (for tea and hot chocolate), cell phones, extra towels from the upstairs bathroom, and a cooler full of ice to the bedroom downstairs. They instructed me to sit on the couch and just watch. There would be no hard work coming from the laboring mommy-to-be—other than the baby birthing kind.

"Wow, that is some bedroom down there. It's no wonder you'd rather be down there than up here. That room is gorgeous. We'll have to light all of those candles." Diane knew great home decor when she saw it.

"Could you light the incense also?" I asked from my designate seat. "I love have the smell of lavender floating around."

"Of course," Diane replied before rushing off to do just that.

Sam came back upstairs and said, "Everything is ready now. Is there anything else that you think you will need?"

"Just make sure all the windows and doors are locked. I know, don't look at me like that. It wouldn't stop a determined vampire, but it makes me feel better. Hopefully it would slow them down enough to alert us to the fact that they're here."

Sam nodded and went off to do just what I'd asked. She came back a few minutes later to let me know that everything was as locked as it could be. It appeared that anything that could have been done was done, so we went downstairs.

I locked the bedroom door behind us. Alex had four locks on the bedroom door and they were all very strong, heavy-duty designs. With those on top of the heavy oak door, I was pretty sure that we would have a fighting chance if someone came banging to get in.

Everyone started putting things where they wanted them to go and we settled into the bedroom. Sam was setting out the contents of her black doctor bag. Francis was layering towels and blankets all over the bed. Diane was plugging up the microwave and setting the clock on it.

I heard Francis mention something about having less than optimal reception on her cell phone. Then, Sam said it didn't matter because we wouldn't be calling anyone. Diane looked at her phone and said that she had a full signal and it must be Francis' service provider.

I sat down in one of the Queen Anne chairs that I'd brought from my grandmother's house months ago. I sat there and listened to the chitter-chatter of these ladies—two were my best friends and the third had been entrusted with my secret—and I realized that everything was perfect (aside from the killer vampire out there somewhere gunning for me). The only people missing were Alex and my mother.

The passing thought of my mother made me miss her. She should be here helping me through the birth of my first child. I thought back on the last words she had spoken to me. She had said something about me not being alone and how I would know the love of a mother for her daughter. I wondered if she knew that I was pregnant. I hadn't even suspected that I was pregnant when she died in my arms.

She would have been so thrilled to become a grandmother after all these years. She'd always aggravated me to get married and spit out some pups, but I never wanted to. Now look at me—pregnant and married. Of course it isn't the ideal situation, but neither would have been the arranged marriage that my pack had tried to force me into.

I was startled out of my reminiscing by a sudden contraction. This one was much stronger and lasted nearly double the amount of time that the others had. Sam came over and felt of my stomach before checking the baby's heartbeat.

"Everything seems to be progressing beautifully, so far. The baby seems to be tolerating the contractions very well. Are you feeling alright?"

"Yes, I'm fine. At least while I'm not having contractions. Those things hurt more than I expected."

Diane chuckled and mumbled something about waiting to see what was to come. I shot her my traditional *Go to Hell* look and she shut up. Sam finished poking and prodding me before going back to getting her supplies ready. I started wishing that there was a television down here. I wondered why Alex never brought one down. I'll have to remedy that problem later.

Just then, another fierce contraction came my way. "Oh hell, here comes another one!" I shouted to the room.

Sam came running. "Already?" She kneeled down in front of the chair and asked to do a check. I agreed. "Oh my goodness, Fiona, you're already seven centimeters dilated and one hundred percent effaced!"

I must have looked at her like she was speaking a foreign language because she explained a little more. "You have to get to ten centimeters and one hundred percent effaced for the baby to be born. This means we won't have much longer before you get to a ten."

Panic started to set in, "Noooo! Not yet!" I stood up and started pacing frantically. "Alex isn't back yet! It's only been an hour! We need more time! He'll be back! I just know he will!" I feared that I wouldn't be able to do this without Alex by my side. And I didn't really want to try without him.

Chapter 18

Once I left Fiona's side, I took to the sky and headed straight to the abandoned warehouse that Sebastian had held me prisoner in the night before. I would have my revenge; one of us would not be leaving there tonight. I hoped with all my soul that he would be the one to lose his life tonight, and not I.

It would normally take close to an hour by automobile to reach Sebastian's warehouse from the cottage. But since I can fly with such high speed, I made it in a matter of minutes. I have noticed that my speed has been slowing down with the more regeneration of my dead cells though.

I feared that in no time I wouldn't be any faster or stronger than an average human male. I would probably lose my power of flight, in time. But, I hadn't told Fiona any of this and didn't plan to do so for a while longer.

I lowered myself to the roof of the warehouse as silently as possible. If Sebastian was here he would know that I had arrived, but I didn't want to give away my exact location just yet. I slipped in through a hole in the roof and descended to the floor. I glanced around and sniffed the air. I had been completely out of it when Fiona rescued me, so I needed to find my way back to where Sebastian had held me captive.

I discovered Sebastian's scent with a light touch of Serena's lingering in the background. They must have been here for quite some time before making their presence known to me at the wedding. I listened closely and heard what sounded like grinding metal, so I followed it.

I kept to the shadows—which was fairly easy since the only light in the warehouse were the beams flowing from the silvery moon. I found a door with stairs leading down into a lower level. I listened and heard the grinding sounds coming louder and could smell Sebastian's scent even stronger, so I knew I was going in the right direction.

I slipped down the stairway as quietly as possible. I had no doubt that Sebastian knew I was coming and had been preparing for my return since my escape. The grinding metal was probably him sharpening some sort of weapon, while building his determination to kill me as soon as he laid eyes on my carcass.

I came to a room that looked like a kitchen area. Sebastian wasn't in here, but I did notice a puddle of blood. Upon closer inspection, I discovered that the blood had been Fiona's. She never mentioned losing this much blood. I sniffed the area thoroughly and found the scent of Diane in a corner and the scent of Serena right on top of Fiona's blood.

It appeared that Serena had been the cause of Fiona's blood loss. I was glad that Fiona had dispatched her. The world would be a much nicer place without the likes of Serena St. John!

I made a mental note to ask Fiona about the blood when I returned, then I followed Sebastian's scent out the door and down a long corridor. The corridor was lined with numerous doors on each side, but I knew that I didn't need to open any of them. At the end of the hallway there was another door. That was the one I had been looking for. I vaguely recalled standing there with Fiona and seeing Diane come running from the room I had just left.

I slowly opened this new door and peered down into a black pit leading to an even lower level. You couldn't see anything past the first five steps, so you just had to hope that there was more down there. Luckily for me, I just hovered above the stairs until I reached the bottom landing.

At the bottom of these stairs I found yet another corridor that wasn't as long as the first, but was lit with torches lining each side. You could tell that these torches had only recently been lit because the wicks weren't burnt down more than a quarter of an inch. I could smell Sebastian's scent the strongest down here. I knew that I was certainly in the right place.

I saw a door at the other end and heard the grinding noise coming from behind it. I walked slowly toward it; each step was a step closer to the unknown. Would I be able to defeat Sebastian? Would I be able to go home to Fiona? Would I see our child be born tonight? Had she already been born in my absence? How would all of this end?

I stepped over the pile of ash that Fiona had told me was Serena. After a moment's thought, I step back and kicked the ash. I watched it fly all over the corridor, flying to and fro. The dust scattered into the air like a swarm of termites. Good riddance! She had been nothing but trouble in her life, and even worse in her afterlife.

As soon as I reached the door, I knew that I should have come into this battle armed with more than just my good looks and strong wit. I was standing there trying to decide what my next move should be when I heard, "Alexander... I know that you are there. Come out and face the grim reaper." I slowly pushed the heavy wooden door open and stepped through, only to come face-to-face with the person I had journeyed here to destroy.

"Ahhh, there you are. Won't you come and join me for a little evening fun?" You could hear the slyness in his voice.

Sebastian was standing over a grinding wheel sharpening a blade as long as a leg. I remembered seeing that sword once before. About seventy-five years ago he used it to murder another vampire that we had known. It had been someone that I had grown to love, someone that had taught me more than any other vampire had, someone who had shown me that we weren't all vicious, murderous fiends of the night.

150

I sneered at the monster before me, "Fun? You're in the mood for fun? Well, then I've come to the wrong place because I'm not here for anything more than the scent of death."

Sebastian laughed his laugh of amusement. It was the laugh that shows everyone around him that he doesn't believe a word that just came out of your mouth and no one else should either. It was the laugh that patronizes every thought in your mind that could possibly become vocalized to the world around you.

I walked over to Sebastian's grinding wheel and laid one hand on it, forcing it to stop against its will. Sebastian didn't seem to mind my interruption; he just stepped back and admired his handiwork on the shiny, sleek metal. His calmness annoyed me more than his stupid laughter.

"Are you ready to do this?" I asked in my own calm, cool, and collected tone of voice.

"Why the rush, my old friend? Wouldn't you rather take a walk down memory lane and enjoy your last few minutes on this earth?" He hadn't even released his gaze on the sword to look at me while he spoke. Such an arrogant bastard!

"And after I dispose of you, I will go enjoy myself with that lovely bride of yours. I'll bet that she enjoys her time with me far more than she ever has with you. Heaven only knows what kind of tortured plain-Jane sex you've thrust upon that poor creature. She might be a disgusting forest animal, but I don't mind when they look like that. Hmmm..."

"What? Nothing to say? No tips on satisfying the woman who is carrying your child? You must have hit it at least once in order to impregnate her with your spawn from hell. I'll make sure to take realllly good care of that little gem when she arrives. It is a girl, right? I certainly hope so because I'd love another little concubine to..."

My blood was starting to boil. I was beginning to see red. I would make sure to break his fucking mouth just for that comment. I flew straight at him, turned quickly, and kicked him square in the mouth with my booted foot! It was like slow motion because I saw tooth after tooth fly from his mouth and watched blood spray across the room. See? I told you that I'd break his fucking mouth!

Sebastian dropped his sword as soon as my foot came in contact with his mouth. I spun around and scooped it up before he had even fallen to the floor. I swung the sword right at his head, but he moved fast enough to escape its blade.

He was back on his feet in a flash and I was coming for him. He was backing into a corner, I swung and he ducked. "I will kill you before the night is over, Sebastian," I stated matter-of-factly.

"Oh, is that right?" Sebastian flew up into the air and kicked the sword from my hands. It landed on the other side of the room with a *thud*. "You still thinking that you'll kill me?" he asked.

I snarled and lowered my fangs. It was time for hand-to-hand vampire combat. Sebastian took the hint and readied himself for the type of savage battle that all vampires know how to fight. We were considered demons after all. And demons know how to tear other beings to shreds.

If you have ever seen a rabid dog fight, that is as close as you can get to imagining a vampire battle. It's savage, bloody, painful, and cruel. It happens so fast that all you can really see are body parts

152

going in all directions. There's snarling, growling, and snapping. There's blood spewing to all corners of the room. There's flesh being torn from flesh and bones being broken. The battle between Sebastian and I was no different.

We circled one another, growling and snapping, just waiting on the other to make the first move. "Come on Alexander..." he hissed. "Do you really think that you can win? You've never been strong enough to defeat me in the past!"

"Tonight will certainly surprise you then, won't it Sebastian?" I growled.

"NOOOOO..." he shouted before charging at me like a Roman soldier in a battle to the death.

I couldn't get out of his way fast enough. He grabbed me by the throat and flew me up against a wall. His grip was tight enough to crush my larynx. The pain was excruciating, but no where near as bad as the last time he had attacked me and left me for dead. I knew that I would have to think fast in order to reduce the chances that an attack like that would happen again.

I punched him in the face and witnessed his newly healed jaw break again. That caused him to release his grip on my throat just enough for me to twist away from his grasp. I flew around behind him and kicked him into the very wall he had previously held me against. His head crashed into the wall and his skull broke before bouncing back off of the wall like a basketball.

I flew over and pinned him face-first against the wall. I punched him in the back, the ribs, the head, and everywhere else that was easily accessible from behind him. Then, I slid up close—my body pressed up against his—and whispered in his ear, "Whose going to die tonight?"

I could see the fear in his eyes. I'm sure his mind was running all types of scenarios through it, just trying to figure out a way to escape me. I had the full force of my body against his and his hands were pinned in front of him between the wall and his own body. He was stuck.

"Maybe next time you should refrain from threatening a man's wife and child. Maybe next time you should act like a civilized man, instead of a murderous fiend. Maybe next time..." I paused. "Oh wait, there won't be a next time!"

I grabbed his head and jerked it to the right before ferociously ripping into his neck. His blood was cold and slow moving. I couldn't remember ever feeding from Sebastian, even though our paths had crossed in numerous ways over the last one hundred and twenty-one years.

I took enough to slow his heart, even more than a vampire's normally slow rhythm. He was on the verge of being drained when he made a sound. I couldn't quite make it out, but it was something.

I released my grip on his neck and asked, "What? Did you have some last words?"

In a voice no higher than a whispering child, Sebastian replied, "I fucked your wife and she enjoyed every minute of it."

On the verge of death and this man could still find the strength to piss me off! My anger suddenly got the better of me. I spun him around and repeatedly punched him in the face.

Unfortunately, he wasn't as weak as I had perceived him to be. He retaliated with a kick to the groin and I instantly fell to the ground—which was a long fall since I'd been holding him against the wall about eight feet off the floor. I fell with a thump and felt a couple of ribs crack in the process.

I watched Sebastian rush over to his sword, scoop it up, and return to where I was crumpled up in agony. He cackled and raised the sword high above his head. "What was that you said about killing me? Did you really think that you would be the last one standing? Well, you were sadly mistaken Alexander!"

I saw the sword being lowered as fast as Sebastian could manage. I knew that I needed to move, but wasn't sure if I could. The sword was only inches away from my throat when I rolled away. The sword had kept a handful of my hair as a memento.

I scrambled to me feet as Sebastian came charging me with his blade of death and a war cry that would shame even the best Viking of the past. His face was twisted in fury and his mouth was snarling like a rabid dog. I stumbled backward, but managed to keep my footing. I took to the air and Sebastian followed. My confidence was quickly waning.

I flew out the door to the chamber and headed out of the building. Sebastian was giving chase and, even in his weakened state, managing to stay close on my heels. I flew up the stairs, down the second corridor, through the kitchen, and then up and out of the building.

Once out in the moonlight, I felt less confined and more powerful. I turned around and saw Sebastian coming straight for me.

As soon as he was close enough, I ducked and nailed him right in the stomach. He yelped and went flying backwards.

"Ah, what's a few broken ribs between friends?" I sneered through groans while grasping my own tender bones.

I watched as he fell onto the roof of the warehouse. The roof gave way from the force of his fall and his body dropped inside. I waited a moment to see if he would come flying back out. When he didn't, I flew in through the hole and planned to finish this.

I fully expected to see him lying there on the floor, writhing in pain, but the only thing lying there was a pool of his blood. My eyes darted around the room, scouring every corner that he could possibly be hiding in. I used every sense I had at my disposal to locate him, but...

He was gone! And I had a good idea where he was headed...

Chapter 19

Sam and Diane helped ease me into a warm bath. Sam said that the water should help with the contractions, but I wasn't feeling any difference yet. I was lying there in a tub that I had planned to only use as a shower and wishing that I was in the one upstairs because it would at least be deep enough for the water to cover my protruding stomach, when I heard a banging outside the door.

I sat up straight in the tub and waited to see if anyone would come in to tell me what was going on or if the banging would happen again. Nothing happened, so I shouted for Diane. She rushed into the bathroom and shushed me. "There's someone banging on the bedroom door," she whispered in hushed tones.

"Is it Alex?" I asked hopefully.

"I don't think so. Alex would have said that it was him and to let him in. Besides, this person is banging with the determination, and desire, to do something terrible to the people within. It has to be HIM!"

"Calm down, Diane. Just breathe. First, help me get out of this tub. It's not helping anyway."

Diane helped pull me into a standing position, but then we had to wait for a contraction to pass before I could step out of the tub. Diane just stood there and allowed me use her body as a prop while I dripped water all over her nice clothes.

"Don't worry about it, sweetie. I'm a mom. I don't wear anything worth more than twenty bucks, or else my kids would surely destroy it." The chuckle that her statement induced made my contraction hurt even more, but it couldn't be helped.

Once I was out of the tub and wrapped in my favorite pajama shirt (which was actually Alex's, but he never wears it anyway), Diane helped me walk out into the bedroom. I sat on the edge of the towel-covered bed and we all just waited. Everyone was seated and staring straight at the door at the top of the stairs. It was so quiet that I looked around to see if everyone was holding their breath, because I was!

"Does everyone remember the escape plan?" I asked in whispers. All of the ladies nodded, but didn't speak a word for fear of discovery.

158

Just then, there was another forceful banging on the door. The person on the other side was pounding so hard that you could see the door jumping with each strike. I hoped that the locks would hold long enough for us to get out of here, if need be. I still had faith that Alex would take care of the situation momentarily.

I motioned for all three ladies to join me on the bed. Diane sat behind me so that I could lean back on her. Sam sat on my right and Francis was on my left. I was having another contraction, but I had to be quiet about it. Diane massaged my shoulders and Sam checked my pulse. Francis proceeded to check the baby's heart rate. All was going well, except for the monster right outside the room.

The pounding passed as soon as the contraction did. "It will be all right," I told the ladies. "We just need to wait on Alex." It had been just over an hour and a half since Alex left and I didn't know how much longer I could hold this child in.

"Do you think we should, maybe, go ahead and leave? I don't like the idea of just hanging out here... waiting for someone to attack," Diane declared.

"Yes, yes, I think we should..." Francis stammered before jumping off the bed and grabbing her cell phone. "I think we should get out of here! I can't just sit here..." She started pacing the room. It appeared that Francis wasn't as calm and collected as we previously assumed.

"Calm down Francis. You knew what you were coming into before you agreed to help out. I'll not have my best assistant freaking out." Sam was not very thrilled with her assistant's current state of mind.

Francis continued to pace and ramble on about fleeing. She started to get pretty loud. As soon as the banging started again, Francis screamed and ran for the escape door.

Sam ran after her as fast as she could, and then she did something I never would have imagined seeing Sam do. She tackled Francis from behind and took her down to the floor! They wrestled around for a moment until Sam gained the upper hand and applied a strong dose of reality with a harsh slap across Francis' flustered face.

"Shut up, Francis! You will stop this bullshit now! Snap out of it or you're fired and I'll make sure you never work for another reputable doctor again!" Sam was pissed.

Sam was straddling Francis and didn't have any intentions of letting her up until she agreed. Francis calmed down, looked at Sam, and then glanced over at Diane and me on the bed. She slowly nodded in defeat to the overpowering doctor above her.

Sam removed herself from Francis' body and helped her assistant to her feet. She made her apologies and we all thought it was over. Until Francis hauled off and decked Sam right across the jaw and made a mad dashed for the exit.

We were all screaming for her to stop, but I was in no position to stop her and Sam was too stunned from the strike. Diane jumped off the bed from behind me and ran like a crazy woman across the room and out the door. Sam climbed onto the bed with me and we hugged each other tightly.

We could hear Diane screaming for Francis to stop. Then we heard a thump (which I assumed was Diane knocking Francis to the ground) and then there was a lot of screaming. I looked at Sam and she looked back at me. We knew that someone was gone... but who?

"Go see if Diane is still in the tunnel!" I demanded of Sam.

"But, I can't leave you hear all alone. What if something happens to me? Who will care for you?"

"Please, just go look! If you won't, then I will!" I started trying to climb up off of the bed.

Sam reluctantly agreed and began to walk slowly toward the door. Her hand was creeping toward the handle when the door suddenly flung open and in stumbled Diane. Sam jumped back from the surprise and then quickly caught Diane before she feel to the floor.

"He's out there! He took Francis! I grabbed her leg before she made it out the other door, but it was too late!!" Diane screamed frantically while lying there on the floor.

"Shhh. Let's just get you off the floor," Sam said while trying to get Diane up on the bed next to me.

"But, she's gone! He took her! She had the outer door open and was nearly outside when he just swooped down and took her right out of my hands!"

"Did you at least get the outer door locked back?" Sam asked nervously.

Diane took a deep breath and gulped down a cup of water that Sam handed her before nodding and replying, "Yes. I locked it back. I didn't want him coming in here after he was finished with her! Why the fuck was she being so stupid?"

Sam shook her head in despair. "She was scared, and fear makes us do stupid things. I should have known better than to bring her

161

here. I should have just come alone. I knew that Diane would be here. I didn't need Francis." Tears started flowing from Sam's blue eyes. She sat down in a nearby chair and wept.

Diane and I sat there and allowed Sam to have her moment of sadness. I helped Diane wipe some grime from her hands and suffered through another contraction. But, this quiet moment didn't last long.

The banging began again. Then it stopped and we could hear things being broken upstairs. There wasn't anything valuable, but I hated to think that all of Alex's things were being ripped to shreds. Then the banging started again.

I couldn't take it any longer. I climbed out of bed—as painful as it was—and started slowly climbing the stairs. Diane and Sam screamed, "What are you doing?" in unison before rushing to my side.

"I'm going to find out what this bastard wants!"

"You already know what he wants!" Diane shouted. "He wants your child, AFTER he kills you!"

"Well, he's getting neither tonight!" I shouted right back. "Just help me up to the damn door!"

"I am highly against this. You need to rest. The birth is eminent and it's going to be hard. You need all the energy you can reserve." Sam was always the doctor.

"It doesn't look like I'm getting any rest. Now does it?" Both ladies shook their heads and Sam mumbled something about just trying to help.

After having to stop for a contraction, I made it to the door. I just stood there and waited. I knew that the banging would begin in another moment. He was most likely circling the house, inside and out, until he finds something that he missed before—an entrance or another stupid person running to escape him.

Sure enough, after a minute, he started banging on the door again. The hits were so powerful that I could feel the floor shaking beneath us. I was ever so grateful that the door was bolted and made of such a heavy material. No doubt that Alex had designed it for just this purpose.

"Sebastian! Stop that damn banging and go the fuck away! No one here wants to visit with you!" I screamed so loudly that my throat began to ache.

The banging stopped and I put my ear to the wood to see if I could hear him. I listened closely and could hear a faint shuffling of feet on the other side of the door. He was definitely standing there.

Suddenly, he started banging again and my head bounced off the door. It scared me so much that it brought on another contraction. It took me so much by surprise that I yelled out in pain and would have ended up down on my knees if it hadn't been for Diane and Sam being there to catch me.

"I think you need to go lie back down." Sam suggested.

I shook my head no and took a few deep breaths to help clear my mind.

From the other side of the door came the voice that I hoped to never hear again, "Yessss, you should go lie back down. We wouldn't want that precious cargo to be harmed. I have plans for her!"

"SHUT UP! You'll never have my child! You fuckin' bastard!" I screamed through the door.

"Ah, such harsh words from the mother of my child. You wouldn't want her to hear such things coming from your mouth about the man who will be raising her. I'm more than thrilled to become the only father that she'll ever know. Well, since her real father was left for dead back at the warehouse. You should have seen the look on his face when the life finally slipped from it. It made me wish that I had killed him long ago."

The anger was boiling now; I would tear his eyes from his head. "You want another beating like I gave you last time?" I shouted as I started trying to get the locks on the door open. "I'll show you just how I feel about YOU!"

Diane and Sam screamed, "NOOOOOO!" before grabbing both my arms and pulling me away from the door while making sure that all of the locks were still intact. On the other side of the door, we could hear Sebastian's sickening laughter.

Suddenly, his laughter stopped! I shook the ladies off of me and leaned in closer to the door again. I pressed my ear against the door, while Diane and Sam braced me in case of another scare, and I listened intently. I could hear someone talking, and not just the lunatic talking to his own alter-ego.

I couldn't make out everything, but I definitely heard Sebastian say that the other person was stupid to protect me. It had to be Alex that he was talking to! I knew that he'd been lying about killing him. I would have felt it if he had died.

I turned to the ladies and whispered, "Alex is out there. We'll be alright now. Let's just go back down and wait this out." They nodded and down we went.

As soon as I made it down the stairs, another contraction came upon me. This one was so painful that I did go down on my knees. I couldn't do anything except stay perfectly still. I was on all fours and Diane was softly rubbing my back.

Once the contraction stopped, I felt a gush of fluid. "Oh hell!" I shouted.

Sam said that it was the bag of amniotic fluid rupturing and that delivery was eminent. My daughter would most likely be born within the next hour or so. Unfortunately, Alex was still dealing with Sebastian and the sun would be rising within the next two hours.

"Please hurry, Alex." I whispered to the floor above me. "Please hurry."

Chapter 20

I flew as fast as I could toward the cottage. I hoped that Sebastian wasn't too far ahead of me. I pushed myself harder than I ever have. I had to reach Fiona before he did. He couldn't find her there, in labor, with only humans to protect her. She was more vulnerable now than ever before.

I was moving along at the speed of a freight train when I caught something out of the corner of my right eye. There was nothing but trees lining both sides of my path, but something was coming toward me at such a high rate of speed that I only spotted it for that one second before it plowed into the side of me. I went flying backwards about one hundred feet before I started falling straight down to the ground.

I heard Sebastian's laughter high above me and opened my eyes just in time to see him dart off again. I climbed to my feet and popped a shoulder back into place before taking to the sky again. My determination to keep my wife and child safe was all I needed to get me through this night.

I was nearly home, without anymore incidents caused by Sebastian, when I heard screams of terror. At first, my old vampire reaction to enjoy the sound, kicked in. But, I quickly snapped out of it and went in search of the person doing the screaming. I was circling my cottage when I spotted someone trying to escape out of the cellar door. It looked like she was fighting someone inside to let her go so that she could get out.

Suddenly, she fell to the ground and I saw Sebastian swoop in faster than a bird of prey to scoop her up and fly away with her. Her screams pierced the quiet of the night like a butcher slicing through beef. Then, just as quickly as they started, her screams ceased instantly. I knew she was dead, but who was it? I hadn't gotten a close enough look before Sebastian grabbed her.

I rushed down to the cellar door to make sure it had gotten closed, but before I got there it was slammed shut and locked. I heard each of the locks latch and was happy to hear that none were overlooked. It appeared that someone was still inside looking after my Fiona.

I took off in the direction that Sebastian had taken the poor soul. I needed to see who it was. I followed the scent and found her body in a small clearing about half a mile from the cottage. Her body was twisted and disfigured. Sebastian hadn't simply drained her, he had made sure to deface every inch of her body. Even her hair had been torn out of the scalp and strewn across the forest floor like pine needles.

I descended to the ground beside the body. Thankfully, I knew that it wasn't Fiona, because the body wasn't pregnant. I had to turn her head around in order to see her face, and I slowly discovered that it was Francis. I was saddened by this revelation, but so very grateful that it hadn't been Samantha or Diane.

I rose to the sky and went toward the cottage. It was time to get this over with. Either I would kill Sebastian or he would kill me. One way or another, this would be finished. One hundred and twenty years of him torturing me, watching me, trying to control me, and now threatening the happiness that I had always longed for, was absolutely enough!

When I arrived at the cottage for the second time, I gently landed on the front porch and listened. I could hear Sebastian inside. He was breaking things all throughout my home. I didn't care about that stuff though. I just wanted to get to Fiona.

I slipped inside the front door with the swiftness of a black cat out for a midnight stroll. Sebastian didn't hear me nor see me come inside. If he had, then I would have certainly known it instantly. I crouched down behind the couch and peered around the corner of it.

The fire was out and there was a chill in the air. The whole room had been destroyed by his fit of rage. Pictures were broken, tables were crushed into kindling and even the food from the refrigerator had been strewn around the room.

I slowly crept through the living room until I came to the corner of the hallway. I stood there, just out of sight, and listened as Sebastian told Fiona that he had killed me and that he would become the father to my child. He would have to kill me for that to become the truth.

I heard Fiona on the other side of the door. She was cursing and yelling and I knew that she was very upset. I could hear the pain in the tone of her voice. If the baby hadn't already been born, then it would be very soon.

I heard a few clicks from the locks on the bedroom door and I began to panic. But, just as quickly, the panic subsided with the shouts from Diane and Samantha and the relocking of the metal contraptions that were keeping them safe. I breathed a sigh of relief and then prepared for the final stand.

I slowly walked out of the shadows and said, "When will you realize that no one wants you around?"

Sebastian turned around with a start, "Ah, so you still live do you? I thought I'd already killed you a few times, but you keep coming back for more. When will YOU realize that you can never beat me?"

"I very well, damn near, beat you back at the warehouse. Or have you suddenly developed a selective memory?" I stepped closer to Sebastian and allowed my fangs to slowly make their appearance.

"Don't come any closer, Alexander. You wouldn't want any harm to come to your lovely little woman, now would you?"

"Now, now, Sebastian, if you could have brought harm to her, we both know that you would have already done so. So don't start acting like you're going to do something that you can't. Remember who designed that room she's safely housed in."

Sebastian bared his own fangs. He stepped closer to me and growled, "That didn't stop me from getting in the other night and taking you during your slumber!"

He was right, but that had been my own fault for feeling secure in my own home. I knew better than that, but had been lax about my stringent security as of late. That wouldn't happen again, especially now that I had Isabella to protect.

"Enough talk! You know that you won't be able to do anything to Fiona. And I won't allow you to lay an eye on my daughter, much less a fang! It's time for you to depart this life and move on to the next. I hope that your time in hell is enjoyable, because that's exactly where I'm sending you!"

With that, I attacked. I jumped onto him. I wrapped my legs around his, wrapped my arms around his, and then dug my fangs into his neck. This time I wasn't going to release him until I knew he was dead. This was no time for a conversation or any last words.

Sebastian screeched like a cat with its tail caught in a car door. He jumped around, tossed from one side to the other, and finally fell to the floor while trying to buck me off of him. I wasn't about to let go this time.

His blood was a little sweeter than earlier because of his feeding session on Francis. But, it was just as cold and just as slow as my previous attempt to drain him. His squirming started to slow and his heart was slowing even more than usual. I heard him mumbling something, but I wasn't about to fall for that trick again.

"I love you, my son," he whispered before I took the last drop of blood from his veins. "I love yo..."

He was dead! He was finally dead! I had beaten him after all these years. He was dead!

I released his body and slowly rose to my feet. I looked down at the creature that had tormented me for over a century. He looked so fragile and harmless, but I knew that he had been anything but those things. And now I was finally free of him. I hoped that he'd gone straight to hell the moment the life finally escaped his body.

Just to make sure he would stay dead, I lifted his body into my arms and took him outside. I grabbed an ax from the tool shed and chopped off this monster's head. And if that wasn't enough, I chained his body to a tree for it to wait on the rising sun to appear. He would be burned into ash by the time I awoke the next evening.

I looked back at the cottage. It was time to go to Fiona. It was time to become a father!

Chapter 21

The contractions were coming faster and closer together. My insides felt like they were on fire. I could hear that there was a battle going on upstairs, but I had no way of knowing who would come out victorious.

I was braced against the back of the bed, with my knees on the bed and my arms crossed over the top of the headboard. Sam was running back and forth between the bathroom and the bedside table. Diane was behind me doing some sort of pressure and massage technique on my lower back and hips.

"AHHHHH! I can't concentrate with all of that racket going on!" I yelled to the room.

Sam walked in front of me and cupped my face with her hands while saying, "Just ignore everything around you. Take your mind into its own place, far away from here. Just try to relax and sway."

"Sway? Sway? Sway to what? There's no music or anything! All I hear is banging and screaming!" Just then another contraction came, "Oh. My. GOD! This hurts so badly!" The pain was so unbearable. My emotions were sitting right on the surface and everything came flooding over me.

"I can't do this! I just can NOT do this alone!" The tears started rolling down my face. I couldn't stop them and they came faster with each released drop.

"Oh honey, you aren't alone." Diane hugged me from behind and laid a hand on my hanging stomach. "You'll never be alone... neither of you."

Her words made me feel a little better, but I still wanted Alex by my side. I didn't sign up to be a single mother... a single, werewolf-vampire mother to a child with super powers, to be exact. How would I be able to do this? I didn't even have my own mother to go to for help, not that she would be able to help anyway. She hadn't been the best mother when my brother and I were little.

"Diane's correct. We will never leave you alone. We are here for you and we will help you deliver this child. We will help you raise her, if need be. No worries." Sam said with a timid smile on her face.

I groaned from the pain, "You two know that's not what I mean. Oh damn it! This hurts so bad."

Suddenly I had a feeling of pressure. So much pressure that, even though I've never given birth, I knew exactly what was happening. "She's coming!" I screamed. "She's coming NOW!"

Sam rushed to my side and asked me to lie down on my back so that she could check to see if the baby was really coming. After the most excruciating moment of her "checking" my insides, she said, "Stay calm, but the baby is turned wrong. She's upside down and she can't be born like that without possible damage to you, her, or the both of you. We'll have to try something to get her to turn around."

"WHAT?" I shouted. The word shocked didn't even come close to describing what I was feeling at that moment.

"Stay calm, Fiona, this sort of thing happens more often than you know." Sam stated matter-of-factly.

"Not to me, it doesn't!" I yelled.

"Why the hell now?" Diane asked. "Why does it have to happen now? She was fine earlier, wasn't she? You checked her over and everything was fine... right?"

"Yes, everything looked perfectly normal, but there is never a guarantee in pregnancy and childbirth. We just never know what will happen. And we all knew that this pregnancy would be full of unknowns," Sam stated while listening to my child's heart beat.

"I need Alex," I said calmly. "I need him now. I need one of you to go out there and find him. Things have quieted down out there... so go! I don't care who it is. But, someone has to go find him." So what if he was in the middle of something—so was I—I wanted him by my side right this minute.

"But, but, Fiona..." Diane stammered along, "what about Sebastian? Don't you want Alex to finish what he's started? What if Sebastian is still out there? I know that it has gotten quiet, but that doesn't necessarily mean victory for our side."

"Diane, look at me! Understand the words that I am speaking to you. I. DON'T. CARE! Go get my husband!" I knew that I was being a bitch, but I was a bitch in dire distress.

174

"No, Diane can't go out there and neither will I. You will be fine. But, we may need to get you to the hospital if we can't turn the baby." Sam was, as always, calm when it came to medical issues.

"FINE!" I shouted like some spoiled brat toying with the lives of her friends.

I stopped insisting that they go find Alex. Sam made me lie on my side, in hopes that the baby would be inclined to roll over. I just laid there and cried. The pain was tremendous and I wanted Alex. I needed to feed so that some of this pain would go away. I'd now been in labor for nearly forty-eight hours and I didn't know how much more I could take of this pain or of being cooped up in here with Diane and Sam.

Just then there was a knock at the door. It wasn't a banging like before. It was a simple "Hi, I've come for a visit" kind of knock.

My sobbing stopped and the three of us looked at one another. Should we open the door? Was it Alex? Or was it just another one of Sebastian's tricks?

I started to get up, but Sam shot me a look that said "don't even think about it" and started up the stairs. She could not have moved any slower if she had been trudging through molasses.

"Go on," I whispered, loudly. But she swatted her hand at me while continuing toward the door.

It felt like it had been one hundred years by the time her hand reached the knob. There was another knock at the door; just as nonchalant as the first one. Sam reached for the first lock, but before she could unlatch it there was a louder, more demanding knock at the door. It made Sam jump and her hand retreated from the lock so quickly that you would think it was on fire.

From the other side of the door we heard, "Fiona! Diane! Samantha! It's Alexander, let me in!"

My eyes grew as wide as saucers. "Let him in!" I shouted. "Please, hurry!"

Sam was still a little cautious, "Are you alone, Alexander? Is it safe?" Her hand had returned to the locks, but she wasn't about to release them from their duty until she felt secure in the knowledge that Alex was the only person on the other side of that door.

"Yes, yes. I've dispatched of the demon bastard, Sebastian. We won't have to be troubled by the likes of him ever again. Now, let me in. I need to be with Fiona—and the sun will be up soon."

Sam looked back at me and I nodded fiercely for her to let him in. I waved my hands at her to hurry up, but she still looked reluctant. "Damn it! Just let him in!" I said. So she finally started unlocking the door. One lock, two locks, three locks and just as the fourth lock was unfastened the door burst open and there stood my vampire husband.

He flew down the stairs and was by my side in mere seconds. His face was covered in blood and his clothes were dirty and haggard. Even his jeans had rips in them. I was so happy to see him alive that I didn't even complain when he rubbed my cheek with his filthy hand.

"Oh, my sweet Fiona," he cooed at me, "are you alright?" He glanced down at my stomach and then back up into my eyes. "How's our little Isabella? Do you think she'll arrive before sunrise?"

176

Sam was standing next to Alex when she jumped into the conversation with, "The baby is turned the wrong way and, therefore, labor is a bit stalled. I will attempt to turn the baby and then we'll see if things progress as quickly as I expect them to. But, if anything goes wrong, we will have to get Fiona to the hospital."

"Oh no. Is it serious?" I could hear the concern in Alex's voice as he spoke.

"No, not yet. This happens all the time, and usually we can get the baby to turn. Then they deliver normally. It's the rare occasion that something drastic happens, but we should be prepared either way."

Alex nodded to Sam, she headed to the bathroom to wash her hands for the millionth time and Diane was sitting in a chair off in the corner taking in the festivities. I was lying there, on my side, waiting for all of this to be over with. Then, a monitor started beeping and Sam came running to my bedside.

She checked the monitor's results frantically. Her face was full of worry. Diane jumped up from her station and rushed to Alex's side.

"What's going on?" he asked.

"It's the baby. Her heart rate is dropping! We have to get her out now!"

Chapter 22

All I could do was stand there as Samantha pushed me out of the way to gain full access to Fiona and our child. I stood there feeling as helpless as a fungus on a tree stump. Then I offered the only thing that I had to give, my blood.

"Do you want to feed, my sweet?" I asked as she was lying there preparing for Samantha to do her magic. She was in so much pain that she couldn't even speak. She nodded slowly, so I glanced at Samantha and she also nodded in agreement.

"I am going to attempt to turn the baby. I want you to stay beside her and let her feed. This is a painful maneuver for most mothers, so hopefully the blood that you will give her will be enough to take the edge off."

I climbed onto the bed beside Fiona and offered my arm to her eager mouth. Her face was tear-streaked and her cheeks were flushed. Her hands rose to grasp my wrist and I noticed that she was shaking from the exhaustion... and possibly from fear of the unknown.

"Ok, Fiona. Try to stay relaxed. I'm going to go ahead and attempt to turn the baby. We need to hurry before her stats decline any more. You may feel a lot of pressure, but hopefully Alexander's blood will lessen that for you." Samantha lifted Fiona's shirt and bared her round stomach.

She proceeded to apply a gooey substance and rubbed it all over Fiona's stomach. "Are you ready?" Fiona nodded. "Alright, go ahead and begin."

Fiona slowly bit into my wrist. Her fangs pierced my flesh slowly and precisely. As she attached her lips to my wrist and began to draw the drug of her choice from my body, I saw the expression on her face change from fright to relief, and then to pure ecstasy.

I nodded to Samantha and she began an odd display of strength and coordination. She slid her hands around on Fiona's stomach, all the while pressing in just deep enough to catch hold of my daughter's little form. She pushed, pulled, and gently tugged at the little being inside of my wife until she had gotten Isabella turned around into the correct position for delivery.

"Now lets see if that little lady will stay put long enough to be born into the world around us," Samantha said through deep breaths from the exertion.

Fiona hadn't even moaned during the procedure. She had the most serene look of relaxation on her face that I hated to interrupt that. Luckily, I wasn't the one who had to do it.

"Fiona. Fiona! It's time to get your daughter out of there." Samantha nodded at me and I rubbed Fiona's hair back from her forehead in an attempt to gain her attention.

Fiona looked up at me and I smiled back. I could feel her hold on my wrist lighten and she slowly pulled herself out of the hypnotic state that vampire blood can incite. I leaned in close and kissed her forehead.

She looked around the room and asked in a more energetic voice, "Is it over? Is she in position?"

We both looked at Samantha and she nodded before adding, "Yes, and now it's time to get this over with. Alexander, do you have time to see your child born, or do we need to vacate the premises so that you won't be in harm?"

I could feel that the sun was near, but I wanted to see my child arrive into this world. I wanted to see if she had her mother's nose. I wanted to hold her in my arms before I had to fall under the spell of a vampire's dead sleep.

"I should be fine, as long as it happens soon. The sun will start rising in a matter of minutes."

"Ok then! Diane, you stand beside Fiona. Alexander, you slide behind Fiona and help her into a reclining position." Samantha was

180

positioning herself at the foot of the bed. She threw Diane a fresh towel and instructed, "Diane, you hold onto that. That's what we'll wrap the baby in when she arrives."

I slipped behind Fiona, just as Samantha had insisted, and laid her head back against my chest. Then I realized that I was still filthy from my battle with Sebastian, so I stripped off my torn and tattered shirt and threw it in a nearby waste basket. Unfortunately, with the sun on the march, the shower I longed to have would have to wait until the next night.

Fiona's top was barely clinging to her after all of the struggles she'd endured throughout the night. I longed to tear it from her body and have our daughter arrive to her parents in the same state of self-exposure as she would be. Instead, I slipped my hands under the top and laid them on Fiona's stomach. I could feel the heat from our child radiating from within the womb.

I noticed some strange places on her stomach that hadn't been there before. I pulled back her top a little and noticed four round marks on one side of her stomach. They were in a row and were similar in shape to fingertips. This must be why Fiona's blood had been on the floor in the warehouse. Serena had tried to rip our child from her womb! If Fiona hadn't already killed that whore, I would have certainly done so after finding out about this.

My attention was quickly reverted back to Fiona when I felt her stomach start to harden up. The firmer it became the more that Fiona's breathing increased in speed and the more that her brow began to furrow. Samantha asked if she was contracting and Fiona nodded. Samantha laid her own hands on Fiona's stomach and confirmed that there was a contraction in the works.

"Ok, Fiona... PUSH! PUSH NOW!" Samantha was using her hands to brace the tender flesh that our child was forcing her way through.

Fiona grabbed both of my forearms and squeezed like her life depended on it. I could feel her mid-length fingernails digging their way into my vampire flesh. It stung a little, but I only noticed it for a second.

"More, Fiona! Push! I see her head!" Samantha's voice was full of excitement and wonder.

Suddenly, Fiona released her grip on my arms; her whole body went limp and then she started convulsing so violently that I thought she would surely fall off the bed. "Samantha!" I shouted. "What the hell is going on?"

Samantha jumped up from her seat, but before she had time to even think about what to do (much less do it), Fiona's body started glowing. I had never seen her do this before, but it resembled the description that she gave me for the time she had destroyed her pack council members. I laid her back on the bed and retreated from her touch as quickly as I could.

"Stand back!" With her recount of the wolf council's death soaring through my mind, I shouted, "We don't know if this is dangerous!"

Fiona's whole body was glowing so brightly that we had to shield our eyes from it. Her skin was almost an intense white light, while her hair was a cooler shade of yellow. I watched as the light started

182

to fade from her head, slowly down her face, over her chest and then it stopped over the baby's position inside her body. Then the same thing happened from her toes, up her legs and again settling over the baby.

It appeared that Isabella was absorbing her powers from her mother before being delivered. As the light decreased, I was able to come closer to Fiona. The convulsing stopped and Fiona was lying on the bed, unconscious.

Diane and Samantha slowly crept closer until we were sure that it was safe again. Diane took a quick swipe at Fiona's arm to make sure that touching her wouldn't burn any of us. "She's cool to the touch. I think it's safe," she muttered.

Samantha went back to her station and I carefully slipped back behind Fiona. I rubbed her cheek and whispered in her ear to awaken her. She slowly regained consciousness, but was terribly groggy.

Fiona's stomach was glowing from the inside out. Kind of like when you put a flashlight against your arm and it looks like you're glowing red—only a substantial amount brighter than that. The skin on her stomach was so bright that we could make out the complete outline of the baby's body; even her fingers and toes!

Fiona's body started stiffening up again. I heard her moan and felt her grasping my arms tightly again. We all watched as the glowing baby proceeded to the exit, in a not so orderly fashion.

"Here she comes, Fiona!" Samantha shouted with caution. "Just a slow, steady push is all we need to get the head out!"

Fiona grunted and groaned while all I could do was sit there and hold her. "You're doing it, my love," I whispered into her ear. "She's almost out. Keep going. It's almost over."

I saw Samantha grabbing the towel from Diane and placing it on the foot of the bed, just under Fiona's legs. Then, she placed a hand over where the baby's head was coming out and said, "Ok Fiona, slow down. Not so fast or you'll tear. The head is almost out! Good, good. Slow."

"Oh, oh! I see her little head!" Diane shouted with perfect amount of self-appointed aunt-ly glee.

Fiona was oblivious to everyone around her. She was in her own world and all that mattered was ridding her body of the child that had consumed her for so long. It was almost over now.

"OK STOP, FIONA! The head's out!" Samantha shouted as she gingerly cradled the head of my daughter while we all had a peek at her scrunched up, red face.

Fiona's body went limp against me. She was breathing heavily and her eyes were closed. Beads of sweat were rolling down the sides of her face. I pushed her wet hair away from her face and neck and then grabbed a near-by cloth to wipe away the salty liquid before it got into her eyes.

I caressed her cheek and kissed her hands. I whispered "I love you" into her ear and she smiled weakly. "Our daughter is adorable. Even with a glowing red face," I told her. To which I was endowed with a little giggle from her lips. I offered my wrist to her, but she refused me and assured me that she was simply exhausted.

184

Another contraction started to build and Samantha continued to keep her hands securely around the baby's oblong head. She looked up at Fiona and said, "Ok, Fiona. Here we go again. One good push and she'll be out. I know that you're tired, but just one more will do it."

Fiona rose up off of my chest, took a deep breath, and went to work. A few grunts escaped her throat, but for the most part, she was silent in her actions. I watched over her shoulder as our glowing child slowly emerged from Fiona's body. First one shoulder, then the other, and with the speed of a deer running through the forest, the rest of her body shot out into Samantha's awaiting arms.

"Oh, dear, she's so warm," Samantha said while trying to hurriedly wrap the baby in the waiting towel without burning herself or dropping the infant.

"Look Fiona, she's adorable," I said to the new mother. But, there was no reply. Not even a little groan of acknowledgement.

Samantha and Diane were busy drying off the baby and suctioning her nose and mouth and making sure she had all of her fingers and toes, all the while being careful not to burn themselves. So no one was paying much attention to Fiona. I slipped out from behind her and laid her back on the pillows. She looked so peaceful. I watched her for a moment...

"Oh, no!" I yelled. "No, not now! She's dead!" I frantically screamed.

Samantha handed baby Isabella off to Diane and ran to my side. She grabbed her stethoscope and listened to Fiona's heart while checking for a pulse in her neck. After what felt like a lifetime,

Samantha declared, "She's not dead. Her pulse is weak and her breathing is less than ideal, but she's fine. It'll take a lot more than childbirth to kill this woman."

Samantha went back to the baby. Then she turned and told me, "We will need to clean her up and I will need you to take her upstairs to the spare bedroom so that I can keep a close eye on her today while you sleep."

Relief washed over me like a waterfall. I breathed a sigh of relief before carefully lifting Fiona's weak body to me. I hugged her tightly and kissed her lips. I couldn't lose her, not after all of this.

After I released Fiona back onto the bed, I walked over to the two ladies who were fondly caring for my new child. They both smiled at me and Diane asked, "Would you like to hold your daughter?"

I nodded and Diane slowly positioned this small, wrinkled, glowing child into my nervous arms. "I've never held an infant," I admitted to the ladies.

"It's alright. You'll be a pro in no time," Diane assured me.

As soon as the baby was laid in my arms, I could feel the heat coming from her tiny, fragile body. She was even warmer than her mother. Her little body warmed me from head to toe. She squirmed a little and made a small sound that resembled a new kitten's mews for its mother.

I sat down in a nearby chair and studied my new daughter. She had a little coating of dark hair on top of her tiny head. It resembled the fuzz of a fresh peach in both quantity and softness.

Everything about her was tiny and precious, like a china doll. Her nose was no bigger than a candy gumdrop and it looked just like a

186

miniature version of mine. She had Fiona's lips. They were just as plump, and I smiled when they appeared to be latched onto an imaginary nipple.

I caressed her glowing cheek and ran my finger around her tiny ear. It appeared that the longer I held her and the more I touched her that the cooler she became. The glow was beginning to slowly extinguish and I was warmer than I'd ever been, since my death, anyway.

She opened her eyes and looked up at me. "Hello little one, I'm you father. You are going to have such an interesting life. You've been wanted for so long and here you are, finally." She squeaked at me and went back to suckling the non-existent nipple.

I chuckled and looked back at Fiona sleeping in bed. I wished that she were awake to enjoy these precious moments. Unfortunately, I didn't have long to enjoy them myself.

I could feel the weariness of dawn arising. I didn't have long before my body would drop where it stood. I handed my daughter off to Diane and turned to Samantha. "We don't have long. The sun is coming up and I won't be of any use to anyone if I'm caught in it and burned to death."

She nodded and instructed me to gently lift Fiona and take her to the upstairs bedroom. I did just that while Samantha started cleaning up the mess downstairs. Diane came upstairs and settled down on the couch with the now sleeping baby.

I placed Fiona on the spare bed, covered her sweat-soaked body with a light blanket and then hoped that she would hear me when I said, "I love you. You have made me the happiest man on this earth.

You have given me the most perfect gift that any woman can charitably offer a man. I hope that I can somehow prove myself worthy of your generosity someday."

I leaned down and kissed her lips before whispering, "Rest well, my love. Enjoy our daughter on this first day of her life and I will be with the two of you at the end of the day."

I left the room and ran right into Samantha. She had an arm-load of blankets and towels and was headed in the direction of the laundry room. "You don't have to clean, Samantha. I'll take care of all that when I awaken."

"No, you won't. You will be spending every second with your wife and daughter for the next few days." She giggled before she continued with, "Besides, blood will never come out if you let it sit there and dry all day."

I kissed my old friend on the cheek and thanked her for everything. "Take good care of her today."

"As if I'd do anything else."

"Before I head downstairs, I have something to tell you," I leaned in close and lowered my voice so that neither Diane nor Fiona could hear. "Sebastian's body is chained up outside, beside that big oak tree beside the tool shed."

A puzzled look crossed her face. "WHAT? Why?" she questioned.

"Don't worry. I dismembered him beforehand. I just want you to make sure that he burns in the sunlight today. He won't be coming back to life with no head, but I want this seen through to the end.

And, since I can't possibly stand out there and keep a watchful eye on the situation, I kind of need your assistance... again."

I quickly glanced out a nearby window and saw the first rays of light begin to brighten the horizon. I ducked back a little into a shadow and Samantha said, "Ok, ok. Just go on downstairs before you become a vampire torch. Fiona would be pissed if I were to let that happen."

"You'll keep an eye on that for me?" I asked.

She nodded, but when I didn't move, she swatted me on the arm and grouchingly shouting, "YES! Now go!"

I went to my daughter's side and kneeled at Diane's feet long enough to lay a gentle kiss on top of my sweet girls head. "Good night, my angel."

"She's a lot cooler now than she was just a few minutes ago. You must have the perfect touch for this little girl," Diane said with a smile on her face.

"Good, I hope that she feels the same about her father when I awaken tonight. Please look after my two ladies while I'm sleeping. And, thank you so much for all of your help, Diane."

"I wouldn't have it any other way. Fiona is the closest thing I have to a sister. I'll always be there for her..." she looked down at little Isabella with such a look of love on her face, "and for this little one."

I laid a kiss on Diane's cheek and then flew downstairs. I remember locking the door behind me (Fiona has a key in case anyone needed to get in) and walking down the stairs. But, I never made it to the bed before the sun's hold washed over me with all the force of a locomotive.

Chapter 23

I awoke to the smell of something burning. It was a rancid smell. Something that made even my cast-iron stomach do flip-flops.

My entire body was aching and I couldn't remember what day it was. I opened my eyes to a room full of sunshine and looked around to discover that I was in the upstairs bedroom. I couldn't remember how I had gotten here though.

To my left, I saw Sam looking out the window. She seemed content so I didn't interrupt her thoughts. To my right, I found Diane sleeping in a chair with one hand thrown over the side of a bassinette.

It all came rushing back to me in that instant. The baby was here! I started to sit up, but the pain inside of me caused a low moan to escape from my vocal chords instead.

Sam turned around and smiled brightly. "So you're awake. I'm so glad to see that. You were in rough shape early this morning and I didn't know how things were going to proceed."

She walked over to the bed and perched on the edge next to me. She laid the cool palm of her left hand on my forehead. Once satisfied with such a professional determination of body temperature, she moved on to the pulse in my wrist. The whole time she was taking sips from what smelled like tea in a mug that was being cradled in her right hand.

"Your temp and heart rate seem to be back to normal. I told Alexander that it would take a lot more than childbirth to keep you down." She smiled as she sat the mug on the bedside table.

I glanced toward the bassinette and asked, "How's the baby?" Then I thought of Alex, "What about Alex? Is everything alright?"

"Oh, everything is fine now that you're awake. Alex cut it close this morning, but he made it downstairs. I don't think he made it to the bed though, because we heard a thump not long after he closed the door behind him. Hopefully he won't wake up too sore from the fall."

I shook my head and tried to hide a small smirk. I could totally see Alex waiting until the very last minute and then passing out in the floor because he didn't have enough time to hop in bed. The imagery was too much to bear without at least a little amusement.

"And Isabella?" I looked toward the snoring Diane—her hand perched precariously on the edge of the bassinette, just waiting for action—and felt a strong sense of love for her.

"The baby is perfectly healthy. All of her stats are perfect and she's been resting peacefully. I hope you don't mind, but we had to give her a bottle earlier. You were still resting and she was hungry. I know that we didn't have time to discuss feeding options during your pregnancy, so I didn't know what you were planning to do." Sam had a look of concern on her face.

"It's ok," I smiled. "Bottles aren't my first choice, but you did what had to be done. I'm sure that we can still begin breastfeeding since you only gave her one bottle. No worries."

"Whew, good! I was afraid you'd be upset." She looked sincerely relieved.

"Can you help me sit up so that I can hold my daughter for the first time?" I asked while struggling to lift my upper body into an upright position.

"Of course!" Sam jumped up, applied gentle pressure to my back, and then pushed heaven only knows how many pillows behind me.

"You'll be sore for a few days, but everything should start going back to normal soon after. Aside from the sleep deprivation, you should start feeling much better soon." She handed me a glass of water and two little pills. "Take these and they will help with the pain."

I did as she instructed and then watched as she slowly lifted this small, squeaking, squirming person from the bassinette. Isabella grunted and made noises that I'd only ever heard come from a dog toy. I could feel my whole spirit lifting at the sight of her.

Sam came around the bed and gently laid my child in the arms that had longed to hold her... mine! It was a perfect fit. Isabella snuggled into the crook of my arm and settled back into her slumber. She was dressed in a pink outfit that had little flowers all over it in multiple shades of pinks and reds. She was wrapped in a matching blanket and even had a cute pink hat adorning her little head.

"Where did all of this come from? I hadn't bought anything for her yet," I asked curiously.

"Oh, well, I kind of had them in my car." I started to protest her purchases, but she stopped me with, "No, don't say anything. Just count them as a baby shower gift. Besides, the child needed something to wear." I smiled brightly and thanked her for her generosity. She then let me know that there were six more outfits just like it, but in different colors, hanging in the closet.

I laughed so loudly at Sam that I woke Diane up. She sat up with a start and instantly looked into the bassinette for the baby. When she saw that she wasn't in there, Diane looked up and discovered that I was awake.

"FIONA! You're awake!" she shouted. "Oh, yuck! What's that smell?" She put her hand over her mouth and nose while looking around.

I looked at Sam and asked, "What is that smell? That was the first thing I noticed when I awoke."

Sam stood up from the bed and walked to the window. She was looking out when she said, "It's Sebastian roasting in the sun."

194

Diane and I both shouted, "What the hell?" so loudly that we startled Isabella and she started to cry. I shushed and rocked her for a moment and she went back to sleep.

"What do you mean by 'it's Sebastian roasting in the sun'?" Diane asked.

"Just what I said, he's out there burning. Alex told me this morning that he had chained Sebastian's body to the oak tree and that he wanted me to make sure that it burned in the sunlight today. So, I've been watching it since then."

Diane rushed to the window and Sam pointed in the direction of the oak tree. "Ewwww! That's disgusting! Is that his head on the ground next to him?" Sam nodded and Diane made gagging noises while walking away from the gruesome sight.

I looked down at the tender face of my new love and relief washed over me. It was really over. Sebastian was dead, Alex was alive, and our daughter was safe and sound in my arms. The only way this moment could have been any better was if Alex had been sitting next to me.

"Did Alex get to hold his daughter this morning?" I looked up, "Before he went downstairs?"

"Oh yes. He was the most perfect new father. He held her, rubbed her little head, and spoke ever so gently to her. I almost cried from the sight of it." Diane was rambling, but that didn't stop her from continuing, "And you should have seen how fast she stopped glowing and cooled down the longer they were together."

Sam shot Diane a glance that meant for her to shut up, but Diane just said, "What? It's true! She hasn't glowed any since then."

"Glowing? My daughter was glowing?" I looked from Diane to Sam, "What kind of glowing? Did anything else happen that I should know about? Glowing seems like it would be something at the top of the list of things to divulge when a mother asks how her child is doing. Don't you think?"

"I'm sorry, Fiona. I wasn't trying to keep anything from you, really I wasn't. I just wasn't sure if you were ready to hear about any of that yet. You have been through so much over the last few days. I just wanted you to enjoy your time with your special little girl before having to worry about what kinds of powers she has, or when she might all of a sudden turn into a fireball again."

Sam came back to the bed and sat down beside me, "I am really sorry. I just wanted you to relax and be a normal new mother for a little while. Is that so wrong?" Her face was covered with sorrow and I didn't want to make her feel any worse.

She had been such a tremendous help through the most scary and unknown months in my life. I couldn't be mad at her. Besides, I know that someone out of these three would have eventually told me about it. It's not like you could keep a glowing baby a secret for long.

"Ok, it's ok. Just tell me what happened. The last thing I remember is you saying that I had one last push and I was pushing. I felt all of the pressure stop and then everything went black."

Sam and Diane began to piece together everything that had happened after that for me. They told me about the seizure I'd had before the birth. They told me about my body glowing so brightly that Alex had forced them to back away from me for fear of injury. They told me about the baby seemingly absorbing all of that energy

196

into her self, and then being able to see her glowing from within my body.

They even told me that Alex had feared I was dead right after the birth. Luckily, I wasn't, but "it was a rough morning and we were worried that we'd have to rush you to the hospital," as Diane stated. I was relieved that they hadn't.

I was told that Isabella had been so hot after her birth, that Sam had to be careful not drop her. But after Alex held her, the heat and illumination ceased and she became a normal infant... for now. I was told about Alex bringing me upstairs and about him telling Sam to watch Sebastian's body.

"And you should have seen him down on his knees telling her good night. It was so sweet. He kissed her little head, and then he kissed my cheek and thanked me for being here. Like I'd be anywhere else besides at your side," Diane gushed and chuckled.

"Thank you ladies, for everything that the both of you have done for me and this little girl over the last few days... hell, the last few months, Alex and I couldn't have gotten through all of this without you two. "

I turned my attention solely to Sam, "Sam, I am so very sorry for your loss of Francis. If you need anything or if her family needs anything, please let us know. I know that Alex would be more than happy to send her family enough money to make sure that they won't have to worry about finances during their time of grieving."

Sam smiled weakly and replied, "She doesn't have any family. She was an orphan. I was the only family she had. I know that Alex would be more than generous though."

Just then, Isabella started grunting and rooting around against my shirt. "Looks like it's feeding time at the zoo," Diane chimed it. "We'll get out of your hair so that you can bond with your daughter. If you need anything, just give a shout. We'll be in the living room." Diane smiled brightly, kissed Isabella's forehead and walked out of the bedroom after leaving a loving pat on my shoulder.

Sam lingered a moment before asking, "Do you need any help getting her situated? I'd be happy to help."

"No, I think we can handle it," I answered with a smile.

"Ok then. Just make sure to tickle her chin a little to make her open wide before feeding," she replied before smiling brightly and closing the door behind her.

I laid back down on the bed, rolled over to my right side, and propped little Miss Isabella on her side facing me. I made sure to stuff a pillow behind her to make sure she wouldn't roll away. Then, we proceeded to introduce each other to the art of breastfeeding.

As I laid there, staring into that lovely, little face, I felt so much love surrounding us. She was beautiful. She had her father's nose and it suited her. Her ears were the most perfect little oval-shaped ears you've ever seen. I took off her little pink hat to discover that she had my hair color. Her small hands were rubbing, stretching, and kneading my breast like a kitten does when it's feeding from its mother.

I snickered a little when she lost suction and made a slurping sound instead. She scared herself with the noise and her whole body shook for a moment. I patted her little bottom and reattached her to the food supply. She settled back into feeding and I laid my head

198

down on the pillow while wrapping one arm up around her head and settling the other hand behind her tiny back.

Then we were asleep...

*　　*　　*　　*

When I awoke, I was all alone in bed. Isabella wasn't curled up against me and she wasn't lying sweetly in her bassinet. I slowly rose from the bed, being careful not to move too swiftly, and drug my poor, tired, sore body into the living room.

Once I crossed into the living room, I saw my beloved seated on the couch while cradling his tiny, newborn daughter in his arms. I stopped and just admired the sight and wished that I had a camera to commemorate this moment in time. I stood there in the shadows and watched Alex coo and whisper to our miracle baby. He was using a tone of voice that I'd never heard any man in my life use toward another person.

Suddenly, there was a knock at the door. I walked into the room and Alex said, "You sit down. Izzy and I will get the door." I grinned at the proclamation that he'd already given her a nickname.

He secured our daughter into the crook of his elbow, led me to the couch, and then headed for the door. There was another rap on the door right before Alex swung it open. He had a smile on his face and was looking down at Isabella when I heard a man's voice, with a foreign accent, say,

"Hello Alexander. I'm Jiang Shin and I'm here to take your baby..."

THE END!

Be on the lookout for the next chapter in

Alex & Fiona's life,

A Twilight Abduction